"Look, I need to make it plain that I don't want anything from you. Right off the bat, I want you to know that," Annie said.

Shane stopped scrunching his hat in his hands and looked at her. "You don't want anything from me. I get that, but I'm fuzzy on the rest. Why are you here? How did you find me?"

Annie crossed her arms and looked at the floor. *Why does this have to be so hard?* she thought. *I'm trying to do the right thing.*

Shane looked down, too. Annie felt his discomfort. The man was six feet tall and as good-looking as the day was long, if a woman liked the blue-eyed cowboy type with a Texas drawl that made every word in the English language sound as soft as a cotton ball.

Oh, yes, he was as sweet and kind as she remembered. And she was about to drop a bomb in his life.

Books by Patricia Davids

Love Inspired

His Bundle of Love #334
Love Thine Enemy #354
Prodigal Daughter #372
The Color of Courage #409
Military Daddy #442

PATRICIA DAVIDS

Patricia Davids continues to work as a part-time nurse in the neonatal intensive care unit while writing full-time. She enjoys researching new stories, traveling to new locations and meeting fans along the way. She and her husband of thirty-two years live in Wichita, Kansas, along with the newest addition to the household, a stray cat named Spooky. Pat always enjoys hearing from her readers. You can contact her by mail at P.O. Box 16714 Wichita, Kansas 67216, or visit her on the Web at www.patriciadavids.com.

Military Daddy
Patricia Davids

Steeple
Hill®

Published by Steeple Hill Books™

STEEPLE HILL BOOKS

Steeple
Hill®

ISBN-13: 978-0-373-87478-1
ISBN-10:   0-373-87478-2

MILITARY DADDY

Printed in U.S.A.

So He said, "Come." And when Peter had come down out of the boat, he walked on the water to go to Jesus. But when he saw that the wind was boisterous, he was afraid; and beginning to sink he cried out, saying, "Lord, save me!"

—*Matthew* 14:29–30

This book is dedicated to Pam Hopkins. If you don't know how much your belief in my talent meant to me all those years ago, let me tell you now. It meant the world to me then and it still does. Thank you from the bottom of my heart.
Oh, and please continue to baby me when I whine about how hard this is.

Chapter One

"**W**ell? Are you going to tell him or not?"

Annie Delmar chose to ignore the question from her roommate, Crystal Mally. Instead she continued folding the freshly laundered clothes in the white plastic hamper on the foot of her twin bed. The smell of hot cotton vied with the dryer sheet's mountain-floral scent.

Hoping to change the subject, Annie asked, "Are you going out with Jake again tonight?"

"Jake and I broke up," Crystal said with an indifferent shrug as she continued to buff her bright red fingernail.

"I'm sorry to hear that."

Annie carried a stack of knit tops to the chest of drawers in the corner. She didn't want to talk about her current problem. It was too soon. It still didn't seem real. Why had God done this to her?

No, it isn't right to blame God. I did this to myself.

Crystal said, "Jake's a loser, like all the guys I date, and don't change the subject. Are you going to tell the guy?"

"I haven't decided." With a weary sigh, Annie closed

the top drawer of the blue painted dresser and stood for a moment with her hands on the chipped and scratched surface.

Crystal plopped down on Annie's bed and leaned back against the headboard. Her short bleached-blond hair framed a face that was pale and too thin. The lacy black top she wore was too tight and, as usual, she had splashed on too much of her cheap perfume. "I don't think he needs to know. Besides, I thought you said he was being transferred overseas in a few months."

"That's what he told me."

"So if you don't tell him soon, how are you going to find him later?"

The door to the room swung inward as their housemother came in with a second hamper of laundry. "That's a good question, Crystal. I'd like to hear your answer, Annie."

Moving back to her bed, Annie began folding her jeans. "If he moves away and I don't know where he went, then I can't tell him anything, can I?"

She glanced at the woman who had taken her in when she had been at the lowest point of her life. Marge Lilly stood with the laundry basket balanced against her hip. On the far side of fifty and slightly plump, Marge managed to look both motherly and formidable at the same time. Her eyes seemed to see right through Annie, but she didn't say anything. After a few seconds of awkward silence, Annie felt compelled to answer the unspoken censure.

"My lack of action would be an excuse to pretend the decision is out of my hands."

"Is that true?"

"No," she admitted with quiet resignation.

"So why not make a decision?" Marge asked gently.

Annie pressed a hand to her stomach to calm her queasiness. "Because I'm afraid I'll make the wrong one."

"And?" Marge prompted.

"And it's easier to do nothing."

"Doing nothing *is* a choice, Annie."

"But not a good one. I need to make *good* choices." Annie had tried to add conviction to her voice, but she'd failed miserably.

"You are in charge of your life, Annie. Just remember, God is always with you, and your friends are here to help."

Annie nodded, but she still felt very much alone and frightened of what the future held.

"Shane, the captain wants to see you on the double."

Corporal Shane Ross tapped the last nail into Jasper's shoe before he dropped the horse's leg, then straightened and looked over the animal's back at his friend and fellow soldier, Private Avery Barnes. "Did he say why?"

"No, but he had that tone in his voice that he usually reserves for me."

Shane grinned. Mentally running over his duties list, he couldn't think of anything he had done wrong or missed. "I wonder what's up."

"It might have something to do with the pretty woman who came in looking for you. If she's your sister, can I ask her out?"

"If I had a sister, I wouldn't let you within fifty miles of her."

"That's not nice."

"But it's the truth." Shane patted the horse's rump and moved to put his tools on the bench at the rear of the farrier shed. He pulled off the heavy leather apron he used to protect his clothing and hung it on a peg. Lifting his coat from the next hook, he slipped it on.

The fire in the forge popped and hissed, adding a smoky aroma to the cold air inside the small stone building. The calendar might say it was the middle of April, but the chilly, damp wind outside made it feel more like winter than spring.

Avery stepped up to stroke Jasper's forehead. "Now that your stint in this unit is almost over, will you be glad to get back to fixing helicopters instead of saddles and horseshoes?"

"I'll admit I'm looking forward to spending a year in Germany, but I'll miss the horses."

"And me?"

"No. You, I won't miss." He would miss Avery and all the men in the unit, but he was more comfortable trading friendly jibes than revealing his true sentiments.

Avery fell into step beside Shane as the two of them left the farrier building. They paused at the edge of the road as three green-and-tan camouflage jeeps sped past. The Army base at Fort Riley, Kansas, bustled with constant activity. When the way was clear, they crossed the street.

The Commanding General's Mounted Color Guard had its main office just south of the large, historic stone-and-timber stable that housed the unit's horses and gear. At the door Avery smiled and said, "Your visitor is a real hottie.

If you aren't interested, could you get her phone number for me?"

Shane gave his buddy a friendly shove toward the stable. "Make sure the wagon wheels get greased today. Our first exhibition is a week from Saturday, and you know the captain wants everything in tip-top shape."

Avery sketched a salute and sauntered away. Inside the tiny office building Shane pulled off his cap and tucked it under his arm, then knocked on the captain's door. When he heard Captain Watson bid him enter, he opened it and stepped inside.

Captain Jeffery Watson was seated behind his large gray desk. The walls of the room were painted the same drab Army-issue color. An assortment of photographs and commendations in plain gold frames added the only touch of color. A faint frown marred the captain's brow above his keen, dark eyes, and Shane wondered again what he had done wrong.

A woman sat in front of the captain's desk, but she had her back to Shane. He couldn't tell if she was pretty or not, but there was something familiar about her.

"Have a seat, Corporal Ross. I understand you know Miss Delmar." He indicated with a wave of his hand the woman sitting quietly before him.

The name didn't mean anything to Shane. She had her back to him, but he could see her dark hair was drawn into a tight braid that reached the center of her back. She was wearing a light gray jacket over a pair of faded jeans. Her shoulders were slightly hunched and she kept her head down.

Shane took a seat in the chair beside her. Glancing over,

he saw her hands were clenched together so tightly in her lap that her knuckles stood out white. He leaned forward to get a glimpse of her bowed face. Recognition hit him like a mule kick to the stomach.

She was the woman from the nightclub. He had spent weeks trying to find her, without success. His satisfaction at seeing her again was quickly tempered with curiosity.

Captain Watson cleared his throat. "I'll be in the stable. You are free to use my office for as long as you need, Miss Delmar. Corporal Ross will let me know when you are finished with this conversation."

"Thank you, Captain." Her soft voice held a definite edge of nervousness.

Captain Watson nodded, then left the room, closing the door behind him.

Shane unbuttoned his jacket. The room seemed hot and stuffy after the coolness of the farrier's shed. He took a moment to study the profile of the woman he had searched for fruitlessly. Now, after almost three months, she was here. Why?

Whatever she wanted, she seemed to be having trouble finding the courage to speak. He decided to get the ball rolling. "Delmar is it? I might have had an easier time finding you if I had known your last name."

Her head snapped up and she met his gaze. "Did you look for me?"

Her eyes were the same deep, luminous brown that he remembered. The same unhappiness he had seen before continued to lurk in their depths. He had the ridiculous urge to reach out and stroke her cheek.

"I went back to that club every night for two weeks hoping to find you again."

She unclenched her hands, folded her arms across her chest and leaned back in the chair. "Two whole weeks. Wow! I'm flattered."

Frowning at her sarcasm, he said, "You left first, remember?"

Her attitude of defiance faded. "I remember. Look, I made a mistake. A big, huge, gigantic mistake."

"You don't get to take all the blame. Nobody held a gun to my head."

"All right, *we* made a huge mistake."

Shane wasn't proud of his behavior that night. "Just so you know, I'm not in the habit of picking up women in bars and taking them to motel rooms."

A tiny smile curved her lips. "Corporal, I could tell. And just so you know, I used to pick up guys in bars all the time for the price of a drink and I've seen the inside of a cheap motel more than once."

Annie Delmar watched the soldier's eyes widen as the meaning of her words sank in. To his credit, he didn't make any smart remarks. She had heard plenty of them in her time, but she never got used to the hurt.

This was so much harder than she had imagined. She wanted to sink through the floor. Maybe she should just leave. That would be the easiest thing to do.

She needed a drink.

No, I don't. I want a sober life. I deserve a sober life. God, if You are listening, lend me Your strength. Help me do the right thing for once.

Drawing a deep breath, she launched into the speech she had worked on for the past week. There was a lot this man needed to understand. "I can tell by your expression that you get my drift. I used to live a very destructive lifestyle, but I'm in recovery now. I had been clean and sober for almost a year when I had a setback. That is no excuse. I made a choice to drink and to spend the night with you when I knew it was wrong."

"What kind of setback?"

His concern wasn't something that she'd expected. "You mean, what caused me to fall off the wagon? It doesn't really matter, does it?"

"It must have."

"Okay, maybe it did, but I've been sober since I left you at that motel. That's what's important. I'm getting the help I need and I'm getting my life back on track."

There was a joke if she'd ever uttered one. Her life was closer to being derailed than on track, but she didn't want this man to think she couldn't handle herself. She would handle this and she would do it the right way, with God's help and the help of others like herself in AA. Still, she found it hard to meet his frank gaze.

"That's good," he said at last. "I hope it wasn't something that I said or did."

She relaxed for the first time in days. "No. You and your buddies came along afterward. You were all so happy about something. You were all laughing."

He had a nice laugh. She remembered that about him even if other parts of that evening were fuzzy.

He pulled his hat out from beneath his arm. She watched him fold and unfold the red ball cap that matched the

T-shirt he wore under his army jacket. She had no clue what he was thinking.

"Our unit had just returned from riding in the inaugural parade in Washington, D.C., and our sergeant had just gotten engaged. She'd be mad if she knew we went out drinking to celebrate. I don't mean to sound like a prude, but I don't normally drink."

"I could tell that, too."

It had been his cheerful smile and his happy laughter that had drawn Annie to him that night. She had craved being a part of that happiness as much as she had craved the liquor.

She cleared her mind of the memory. "Look, I need to make it plain that I don't want anything from you. I want you to know that. I don't want anything from you. Do you get that?"

He stopped scrunching his hat and looked at her. "You don't want anything from me. I get that, but I'm sort of hazy on all the rest. Amy, why are you here? How did you find me?"

"My name is Annie."

"Annie. I'm sorry."

She thought she was done feeling like this. Cheap and disposable. Crossing her arms again, she looked down at the floor. "Don't be. The music was loud. We were…"

Why does this have to be so hard? I'm trying to do the right thing, Lord. Please help me.

Shane looked down and began folding his hat again. "I never was good with names. I forget my own sometimes."

Annie saw his discomfort and took pity on him. The

man was six feet tall and as good-looking as the day was long—if a woman liked the blue-eyed cowboy type with a Texas drawl that made every word in the English language sound as soft as a cotton ball. And he was embarrassed because he didn't remember her name.

"It's okay. It's not like we had any intention of becoming best friends."

Looking up, a slight grin pulled at the corner of his mouth. "My list of friends is pretty short. I'd be honored to add you."

Oh, yes, he was as sweet and kind as she remembered—and she was about to drop a bomb on his life.

"As for finding you," she continued, "that wasn't hard. It's a big Army base, but how many stables are there here?"

"One."

"Right. I called and spoke to your captain yesterday and he told me when you would be here today."

Annie glanced at her watch. She couldn't stay much longer. It was time to get it over with.

This is my step number nine: I need to make amends for the harm I caused. I need to admit the truth.

Was she doing the right thing? She wasn't sure she should burden this man with her news. Telling him wouldn't change anything, but Marge believed that he had a right to know, and Annie believed in Marge's wisdom. She had seen it in action time and time again.

Annie raised her head. She had come a long way in the last year even if she had slipped up one night. She could be proud of what she had accomplished since she'd turned her life over to God. Something good would come of this because it had to be part of His plan.

"Corporal Ross—"

"Call me Shane."

"Okay, Shane, I'll get to the point. I'm here because I'm pregnant."

Chapter Two

Shane blinked once, not certain he had heard Annie correctly. He opened his mouth but closed it quickly without posing the question that dangled on the tip of his tongue.

"Aren't you going to ask me if I'm sure it's yours?" she demanded.

The mixture of defiance and pain in her voice made him glad he hadn't spoken that thought aloud.

"I don't think you would have gone to the trouble of finding me if you weren't sure."

Her attitude softened slightly but not completely. "That's right."

She shot to her feet, clutching the strap of her scuffed black vinyl purse. "Okay, then, I guess we're done."

He stood in surprise. "Whoa! You can't just lay this on me and then scoot out the door."

"Why not? I told you I didn't want anything from you."

"You've just told me I'm going to be a father. I need more than a minute to process that information."

"Sorry, but one minute is all you get. Look, neither one

of us wanted this. We were both looking for a good time, not for a family. My counselor convinced me that you deserve to know. Now you know. From here on out it is my problem and I'll handle it as I see fit."

"I'm not sure I agree with that. What are you going to do?"

"I'm going to leave here and get to my job before I'm late. Have a nice life."

She stepped around him and headed for the doorway. Was she kidding? She had hit him with this brick and now she was going to split? As she started to pull open the door, he reached over her head and pushed it shut with a bang. "Wait just a minute!"

The look she sent him was twice as sharp as the nails he had put in Jasper's shoe. "Take your hand off this door."

"I will as soon as we settle a few things."

She crossed her arms and glared at him. "Such as?"

"Do you plan to keep the baby?"

"None of your business."

"I hope you aren't considering an abortion."

"That is also none of your business."

"If it wasn't any of my business, you wouldn't be here. I'm not sure what I'm supposed to do or what I'm supposed to say, but this isn't just your problem."

She drew a deep breath. "I have to decide what is best for me. You don't get a say in that."

It was plain she didn't want his help or his interference. If she didn't want him involved, wasn't that her right? Past experience had certainly proven he wasn't father material. Why should this woman think differently? She barely knew him and yet she had already made that decision. He pulled his hand away from the door frame. "Okay, you need to do what is best for you. I guess I can understand that."

"Good."

Shane stuffed his hands in his pockets and stepped away from her. "I'm sorry this happened. If there is anything you need…anything…let me know."

"I won't need anything, and you don't need to worry that I'll show up again looking for support for this kid. For what it's worth, I'm sorry you had to find out like this. You seem like a nice guy."

He quickly crossed the room to the desk. Picking up a pen and business card, he scribbled his cell number. Returning to her side, he handed it to her. "This is my number. Could you at least let me know what you plan to do? I really want to know."

She hesitated, but took it from him. "I'll think about it."

Annie pulled open the door and walked out of the office with her heart pounding like a drum in her chest. Her hands felt ice-cold and her legs were barely able to hold her up. She prayed she could make it to her car without falling down. She was bad at confrontations.

Corporal Shane Ross had no idea how much it had cost her to maintain her mask of indifference. At least the dreaded meeting was over and she could stop worrying about it. Now it was time to look ahead and make a plan.

She managed to reach her car. A soldier stood on the other side of her beat-up peacock-blue hatchback, chatting through the rolled-down window with her roommate in the passenger seat. Crystal was laughing at something the man said. Annie glanced back. Shane stood just outside the building, watching her. His face wore a puzzled frown. Who could blame him?

The sudden *clop-clop* of hooves startled her as a soldier walked past, leading two brown horses with black manes and tails. She had heard a lot about Shane's unit from him during their one evening together. At first she had thought he had been teasing about being in the cavalry, but it had soon become apparent that he and his friends really did ride horses in a modern army.

Shane had spoken with quiet pride about his participation in the inaugural parade in Washington, D.C. She could still see his shy smile and the sparkle in his blue eyes when he spoke about it. He hadn't been the best-looking guy in the bar that night, but there had been something about him. In him she thought she had seen someone like herself. Someone without anyone.

Yeah, and look where that got me.

Opening the car door, she climbed in and slammed it shut. If only she could shut out her memories as easily.

Crystal leaned toward her. "How did it go?"

"I'll tell you later."

"Did you see those horses?"

"I saw them." Annie tried twice to get the key in the ignition before it finally slid into place. Her hands wouldn't stop shaking. *Please, please let it start.*

"Private Avery was just telling me that we can have a tour of the stable and even pet some of the horses."

"We don't have time. We're going to be late as it is."

"Come back someday when you can stay longer," Avery suggested. "I'd be happy to give you a private tour."

"I'd like that," Crystal gushed.

The car's temperamental engine turned over. Annie breathed a silent prayer of thanks, then backed out of the parking space.

"'Bye," Crystal called, waving as they drove off.

"Roll up the window," Annie snapped. "It's freezing in here and you know my heater doesn't work."

Crystal did as she was told. "You didn't have to be rude to Avery. He only wanted to let me see his horses."

"It was just another pickup line."

"It was not. Sometimes I think you don't like men."

"I don't dislike them. It's that I don't trust them—and neither should you." If Crystal couldn't see that, Annie wasn't going to waste her breath trying to convince her.

Shane turned away from the sight of Annie's car disappearing down the street. He knew he'd never hear from her again. She had already decided he had no business being a father.

Avery came over to stand beside him. "What did the lady want?"

"I thought I told you to grease the wagon wheels."

"Lee had already taken care of it. Obviously your friend didn't bring you good news."

"She told me I'm going to be a daddy and then she told me to get lost."

"What?"

"Do I have a sign over my head that says *Rotten Parent Material?* Do I have *Loser* written on my forehead?" Shane began walking toward the farrier shed so quickly that Avery had to run to keep up.

"I don't think you really want me to answer that."

"You're right, I don't. Now, go away."

It seemed that Avery couldn't take a hint. He followed Shane inside the building and asked, "What are you going to do about your pregnant friend?"

Tossing his jacket aside, Shane slipped the strap of his leather apron over his head and tied it at his waist. "Annie Delmar wants nothing to do with me. In light of that fact, I'm going to respect her wishes."

Moving back to Jasper's side, Shane bent over and picked up the horse's hind leg. "This shoe needs to be replaced, too. Hand me the clinch cutter and the pull-offs."

Avery walked to the workbench at the back of the room and returned with the requested tools. Handing them to Shane, he said, "You can't drop your responsibilities like a hot rock."

"It's not my call."

"I beg to differ. It certainly is."

"Not according to Annie."

"You have the same rights that she does."

Shane tilted his head to see his friend better. "What do you mean?"

"The law is plain on this. A father has the same rights that a mother does. Well, almost the same. You do have to prove that the child is yours."

Jasper tried to pull his foot away and Shane let him put it down. Ordinarily the big gelding didn't mind having his hooves worked on, but he seemed to sense Shane's emotional turmoil. Patting the horse's side to reassure him, Shane drew a calming breath.

He knew what it was like to be the child waiting for a father that never showed up. "The law doesn't matter. I'm not going to fight Annie so I can force her to let me see my kid every other weekend—or less. That's not what a family is."

Avery said, "This doesn't sound like you. You've always been Mr. Responsible."

"I guess you don't know me as well as you think." Shane picked up Jasper's hoof again and began straightening the tips of the last few nails holding the worn shoe in place.

Maybe never knowing this child would be better than loving him and then having to watch some other man step in and take him away. Only…this was his child. How could he pretend it didn't matter? It might matter, but what choice did he have?

"When I start a family, I'll be married and I'll have a job that lets me come home every night. My kids are going to know who their daddy is."

Crossing his arms over his chest, Avery said, "Your plan is good except for one small detail. You've already started your family."

Struggling to keep his frustration and disappointment from showing, Shane said, "Look, I'm not even sure she's keeping the baby."

"If she plans to give it up for adoption, she'll need your consent or it won't be legal now that she's admitted it's your kid."

"I'll cross that bridge when I come to it." Picking up the long-handled tool that looked like an oversize pair of curved pliers, Shane positioned the tips under the heel of the horseshoe and began carefully rocking it back and forth to pry out the nails without damaging Jasper's hoof.

"I think you're making a mistake, but it's your life."

"Thanks for noticing. Be sure and shut the door on your way out."

He didn't want to talk about it anymore. If he didn't know how he felt about the situation, he sure couldn't explain it to someone else. He needed time alone to think about what he should do, if anything. When Avery didn't move and didn't reply, Shane tugged the horseshoe loose, let go of the horse's foot and straightened to face him.

"Even if I want to take some level of responsibility for this baby, Annie made it very plain that she doesn't want that. I don't even know where she lives or how to contact her to discuss it."

"I don't know where she lives, but I can tell you that she works at the Windward Hotel out on the interstate."

Shane scowled. "How do you know that?"

"Her roommate, Miss Crystal Mally, works there with her. If I'd had a few more minutes, I would have had a phone number and a home address to go with that information. Crystal is a talkative girl, even if she isn't exactly my type."

"I didn't know you had a type."

"I don't, really, but I do shy away from junkies."

"Annie said she is in recovery. She mentioned having a counselor."

"Annie may be clean, but I don't think Crystal is there yet. Believe me, I know the signs. I hung out with a fast crowd before the Army got a hold of me."

"Knowing where Annie works doesn't change anything." Shane walked over to the forge and thrust a metal bar into the coals.

"Maybe not, but at least you know how to find her when you've had a chance to think things over."

He didn't want to think things over. He wanted to rewind the morning and erase the part where a pretty woman with sad eyes had turned his life upside down.

Two days later, Shane rounded the corner of the snack-food aisle at the local Gas and Go and spied Annie paying for her purchase of a large soda. Confronted with the woman he hadn't been able to get off his mind, he simply stared.

She wore a pair of faded jeans with butterflies embroidered in pink-and-white thread at her ankles. An equally faded jean jacket with threadbare cuffs covered a dark pink blouse. Her long braid hung down to the center of her back and swayed softly when she moved. Her silhouette showed only the slightest fullness at her midriff. A casual observer wouldn't know she was pregnant, but he knew. She was carrying his child.

What he should do about it—if anything—had kept him awake most of the last couple nights.

She was searching in the depths of her purse for money to pay for her drink and she hadn't seen him. Should he stay out of sight until she was gone or walk up to the counter as though it didn't matter? It wasn't in him to take the coward's way out. He closed the distance between them in a few steps.

"I'll pay for the lady's drink," he said to the teenage boy manning the cash register.

Annie's eyes flew open wide as she stared at him in shock. Her surprised look vanished as a frown deepened the furrow between her brows. To Shane she looked tired, as well as mad.

Before she could speak, he said, "I didn't think cola was good for pregnant women."

"It's lemon-lime—not that it's any of your business what I drink. What are you doing here?" she demanded.

He felt a tug of admiration for the way she stood up to him. "Picking up a quart of oil for my car and getting a burrito. Not that it's any of your business. How much?" He directed his question to the clerk.

The boy rattled off the price and Shane pulled a ten from his wallet. Annie seemed to be having trouble finding a comeback. After a full five seconds of silence, she said, "I can pay for my own drink."

"Too late." Shane took his change, dropped the coins in the front pocket of his jeans and tucked the bills into his wallet.

Annie pulled herself up to her full height, which wasn't much over five feet. "I thought I made it plain that I didn't intend to see you anymore."

"You did, but Junction City isn't a big town. We may run into each other again." He nodded his thanks to the clerk and picked up the white plastic sack with his purchases.

"I was serious when I said I didn't want or need anything from you," she insisted.

"I know you were." He walked to the door and pushed it open. The bell overhead jangled and the sounds of the street traffic grew louder. "The trouble is, Annie, you forgot to ask *me* what I want to do about our little problem. I do have a say in this, no matter what you think."

"What is it you want to do?"

"I'm not sure yet, but I'll let you know when I reach a decision." He walked out the door and let it swing shut behind him. He glanced back as he stepped into his car. Annie watched him from inside the doorway. She was biting her lower lip.

Shane felt the stirrings of sympathy for her. He didn't want to add to the worries she carried. He wasn't sure what he wanted to do, but he knew he couldn't let Annie Delmar just walk out of his life.

Early Monday morning Annie and Crystal sped into the Windward's parking lot. Pulling around to the area reserved for staff, they both bolted out of the car and rushed in the side door of the building. For once it wasn't Crystal and Annie's poor excuse for a car that had made them late. This time it had been Annie's fault. The sudden onset of morning sickness had stopped her cold just as they were leaving the house.

Inside the building, the women dashed to the locker room, where they quickly changed into gray pin-striped smocks and gray pants. Annie tossed her own clothes and purse into her locker and shut the door. Running a hand over her hair to tame the flyaways, she took a deep breath and followed Crystal into the windowless, drab room that served as a cafeteria and meeting room for the hotel staff. Four other housekeepers sat at one of the tables. Their supervisor was standing at the front of the room.

Mr. Decker looked at the clock on the wall. The hands pointed to two minutes after eight. "I'm glad you ladies could join us." His sour tone made Annie wince.

"I'm sorry, Mr. Decker," she said. "It won't happen again."

She needed to make sure of that because she really needed this job. She would have a baby to take care of soon.

The thought hit her out of the blue: she was keeping this baby.

Sometime between tossing and turning half the night trying to make a decision and now, the answer had been found. This was her baby. She would love it and raise it and give thanks for the blessing every day for the rest of her life.

"All right, let's get started." Mr. Decker was short and as thin as a toothpick. His unnaturally black hair was combed carefully over his bald crown, but his gray pin-striped suit was meticulously pressed with a carefully folded white handkerchief peeking out of his breast pocket. He picked up a clipboard from the table and scanned it quickly.

"We have thirty-two guests checking out this morning. Crystal and Annie, you will take the ground floor of the west wing."

Annie relaxed as he finished giving the other maids their assignments in English or in fluent Spanish for the women who needed it. The west wing was longer and therefore had more rooms, but she knew Crystal would help her if she fell behind. After only a month on the job, Annie still wasn't as speedy as Crystal. Crystal had been a maid at this hotel for over a year.

After morning assignments were finished, Annie loaded her cart with fresh towels and linens and replenished her bottle of glass cleaner. At the first room on the west wing, she knocked briskly. There was no answer. She swiped her key card and pushed open the door as she announced herself. Stepping over the threshold, she stared in dismay at the mess awaiting her.

Trash overflowed from the wastebasket and dirty clothes were scattered around the room. The bedding was piled on the floor below the foot of the mattress. A large pizza box lay open on the table. It was empty, but one upside-down slice had made it to the floor, where the cheese and tomato sauce were still soaking into the carpet.

This wasn't going to be a quick turndown and wipe. She checked the dresser top. Of course the occupants hadn't bothered to leave a tip for the poor soul who had to clean up after them. With a sigh, she began picking up articles of clothing. Her day may have started out badly, but she wasn't going to let it get her down. She was having a baby!

It took her almost thirty minutes to finish the room, but when she'd pulled up the clean spread and tucked it beneath the freshly fluffed pillows, she straightened and looked around with pride. She wasn't the fastest maid, but she always did a good job. There was something satisfying about creating order out of disorder. If only it were as easy to straighten out her life.

By four o'clock she was exhausted and she had earned only a single five-dollar tip. It would be enough to put a few gallons of gas into her car, but she wouldn't be able to get her flat spare tire fixed or put any money aside. The list of things the baby would need almost made her cringe.

In the locker room she sat on the bench and rubbed her aching feet. Closing her eyes, she whispered softly, "The Lord will provide."

She was learning that faith was a tricky thing. Just when she thought she had a firm grasp on it, something happened that made her doubts come back. Things like a day with lousy tips.

Being a Christian isn't about material stuff.

Annie tried hard to keep that in mind. It was about eternal life and about His love. She couldn't know His plan for her, but was it wrong to hope that it might include enough money to get a new pair of shoes?

She glanced at the clock as she waited for Crystal to join her. When her roommate rushed in ten minutes later, her face was flushed and she looked as nervous as a cat in a dog pound. Opening her locker, she grabbed her purse, then tossed her coat and her clothes over her arm. Glancing over her shoulder, Crystal said, "Come on. Let's get out of here."

"Aren't you going to change? You know Mr. Decker doesn't like us taking our uniforms home."

"He's gone for the day. He'll never know. What are you waiting for?" Crystal pulled open the door to the hallway, checked both ways, then hurried to the exit.

Annie followed her, puzzled by her odd behavior. "Crystal, what's wrong with you?"

"Nothing, I want to get home, that's all. I'm meeting Willie in half an hour."

"Who is Willie?"

"I met him last night at Kelly's Diner and I think he's the one. He's so cool. I told him I could give him a lift home after his shift is over in the evenings. That is—" she paused and looked back "—if I can borrow your car? You don't mind, do you?"

"Oh, Crystal." Annie didn't try to hide her disappointment.

"What? This guy could be the one. You don't know him."

"And neither do you."

"Don't be that way. He makes me feel special." Crystal pushed open the outside door but stopped dead in her tracks with a sharp gasp. Just as quickly she relaxed and said, "Oh, it's you."

When Annie came out the door, she saw Shane standing beside her car. Her breath caught in her throat. Dressed in jeans and a dark blue sweater that accented the color of his eyes, he looked far too handsome and exactly like the man she had fallen for that night three months ago.

Calling on all her willpower, she hardened her heart against a sudden and frightening desire to step into his embrace and rest her head on his shoulder.

He nodded at Crystal but walked past her to stand in front of Annie. "We need to talk."

Chapter Three

Shane was prepared for a verbal battle, but to his surprise, Annie didn't tell him to take a hike. She edged away from him, toward her car. He had the distinct impression that she was afraid of him. That was the last thing he wanted.

She licked her lips quickly, then said, "We don't have anything to discuss. How did you find me?"

He smiled, trying to put her at ease. "Let me buy you a cup of coffee and I'll tell you."

"I don't drink coffee."

"Then make it a cup of tea or a lemon-lime soda—anything you want. Annie, I'm not going to go away until we've had a rational discussion about our baby."

He had come here intending to do just that, but now he found himself wanting something different. His motives had been hidden even from himself until he'd seen her face today. She looked tired, sad, vulnerable. That vulnerability was what he remembered most about her. It was why he had looked for her after their night together. It was why he couldn't get her out of his mind.

Now that he had found her again, he wanted to spend time with her. He wanted to get to know her better. He needed to find out if their one bittersweet meeting might have been the beginning of something special.

Crystal shifted from one foot to the other beside the car. "I need to get going. I told Willie I'd meet him after work."

Annie took another step toward the car. "I need to get home."

She was making it obvious that she had no desire, hidden or otherwise, to spend time with him. Shane took a step back and held up his hands. "All right, but I'll be here tomorrow…and the day after that and the day after that. Sooner or later, you're going to have to talk to me."

He watched her indecision play across her face. She chewed the corner of her bottom lip for a few seconds, then she turned to her friend and held out the car keys. "You go, Crystal. I'll be home later. Tell Marge that I went to get a cup of cocoa with Corporal Ross."

Crystal took the keys. "Are you sure you want to do that?"

Relieved by her change of heart, he said, "I'll see that she gets home."

Annie's smile looked strained, but she nodded. "I'm sure. You go on."

Shane worked to keep his elation in check. He didn't know where any of this was going, but at least he was doing something. She was willing to talk to him and he wasn't going to waste the opportunity.

As Crystal drove away, he faced Annie and asked, "Where would you like to go?"

"The hotel has a restaurant. We can go there."

"Fine by me. Lead the way."

It was too early in the evening for the Italian-themed bistro to be busy yet, but the aromas coming from the kitchen were tempting enough to make Shane hope he could convince Annie to have dinner with him. Once they were seated in a corner booth out of earshot of the other customers, he leaned back against the green plaid fabric and smiled to put her at ease. "Crystal told my friend where you and she work."

Annie frowned at him. He shrugged. "You asked how I found you."

"Oh." She rearranged the salt and pepper shakers and moved the green ceramic container of sugar and sweetener packets to the center of the table to form a straight line. She seemed to realize what she was doing and quickly clasped her hands together. The clink of tableware and muted voices from the other diners did little to fill the void of silence.

"So where do we start?" he asked as he studied her face. She was pretty in an exotic way with her long, dark hair and deep brown eyes. Dressed in a simple white blouse with short sleeves and a pair of black slacks, she seemed to want to blend in rather than stand out from the crowd. Her lips were full, and he remembered the way they had softened when he'd kissed her.

Was the sweetness he had tasted that night really there or had it been part of a dream? They were going to have a child together, but he realized he knew almost nothing about this woman. He wanted to know more. A lot more.

She met his gaze. "You tell me where to start. You're the

one who insisted on this meeting. I still don't understand why. I thought I was letting you off easy."

"Easy? You call this easy? Every day of my life I'm going to wonder if I had a son or a daughter. You intend to go your merry way and I'll never know where he is. I'll never know if some other man is reading him the stories he likes or playing catch with him or taking him fishing."

Pressing his lips into a tight line, Shane looked down and struggled to keep the old pain in check. The waitress arrived to take their orders, and it gave him a moment to compose himself.

When she left, Annie said softly, "I'm sorry. I didn't mean to make light of the situation. There's something more going on here, isn't there?"

He was surprised by her perception. Shaking his head, he said, "It's a long story. I don't want to bore you with my ancient history."

"You wanted to talk. I'm trying to listen."

Touched by her compassion, Shane considered how much he should tell her. If he had any hope of convincing her to let him share in the decisions she had to make, he would need to gain a level of her trust. Wasn't that worth exposing a part of his past, even if it was a painful part?

Slowly he began telling his tale. "I was engaged about a year ago. Her name was Carla. She had a little boy named Jimmy. He was the cutest, smartest little kid you have ever met. At four he knew the entire alphabet."

He paused, remembering those happy times, remembering how proud he had been of Jimmy.

"He was your son?"

"No, but that didn't matter. It didn't matter to me, anyway. It was easy to love Jimmy and to think of him as my own. I believed that I was in love with Carla, but it was Jimmy who got me to thinking about making us one big happy family. For Carla it was a different story."

"How so?"

"Jimmy's father had split right after Jimmy was born. He never kept in touch, never paid support—you know the type."

The deep bitterness in his voice momentarily took her aback. "I've met a few guys like that in my time."

"One day he showed up again. Carla decided life would be better for Jimmy with his 'real' father. She broke it off with me, went back to him and they moved away."

"That must have been rough."

"It was. Jimmy didn't know his 'real' father from a hole in the ground. I was the only father figure he'd had in his life. Carla was an adult. She made her choice and I hope she is happy, but Jimmy didn't get a choice. I hope he's happy, but I'll never know for sure."

"So what do you want from me?"

He stared down at his hands clasped together on the tabletop, then looked up and met her eyes. "I keep asking myself that same question. I guess I want to know that you have all you need to make a good life for my son or daughter."

The waitress came back just then with their order. While Shane added a spoon of sugar to his coffee, Annie toyed with the marshmallows floating on her cup of hot chocolate. She hadn't expected him to reveal so much about himself. She hadn't expected to empathize with his feelings of loss or to find herself wanting to comfort him. What was it about him that broke through her defenses?

He had been a one-night stand. She had been with dozens of men in those years when addiction ruled her life and made getting another drink more important than food or shoes, more important than friends or family. The list of loved ones damaged by her sickness and her bitter refusals to get help was longer than her arm.

"Shane, I respect that you want to be involved, I do, I just don't see how I can promise you anything."

"I'm not looking for any promises. I just need to know that both of you are going to be okay."

"I'm okay without your help."

A lopsided grin made a dimple appear in his right cheek. Why did he have to be so cute and so genuine?

"I'm sure you are, but it seems that I'm not. Can't you see some way to…I don't know…to let me give you money to help with expenses?"

Annie's sympathy for Shane splintered like a cheap glass on a tile floor. Shards of it pricked her hard-won self-respect.

"I don't take money from men."

"Oh, man, that's not what I meant. Not at all. I'm sorry. I didn't even think—"

"Fine." She cut him off, wanting only to get home and curl up in her bed with her head under the covers. She started to get out of the booth, but he stopped her by laying a hand over hers on the table.

"Please don't go. I'm a total jerk. Ask anyone who knows me. I put my foot in my mouth fifty times a day."

The sincerity of his plea gave her pause, but it was the

look in his eyes that made her stay. "That must make it hard to march in formation."

He relaxed, a ghost of a smile curving his lips. "I'm lucky—in my outfit the horses do all the legwork."

He drew his hand away slowly. Oddly she wished he hadn't. For a tiny fraction of time she had felt comforted by his touch.

It was ridiculous. She didn't need his help, his money or his comfort.

"Can you accept that I'm a well-meaning, if inept, person?" he asked.

"I guess I can accept that."

"Good. I honestly do want to help. Tell me how."

It would be so easy to give in to his pleading and let him shoulder the responsibility of providing the things she and the baby would need. Things like their own place to live, a crib, even clothes for the baby. But to do that would be like going backward in her recovery.

Once, she had used alcohol as her crutch to make life bearable. She wouldn't substitute that addiction for a dependence on this man, even if it seemed harmless on the surface. Her track record with relationships didn't include any that had been harmless.

"Thanks for the offer, but I think the best thing for both of us is to go our separate ways."

"I have rights as a parent." His tone carried a new determination.

So he wasn't harmless after all. "What are you saying?"

"Under the law, I have the same right to this baby that you do."

"Is that a threat? If you think you can take my baby away, you had better think again. I'm not afraid of you."

He held up both hands and shook his head. "It's not a threat. I'm not saying I would make the better parent." Leaning forward, he clasped his hands together. "I have no intention of trying to take this baby away from you. I'm only saying that I have an equal responsibility to take care of him or her."

She wasn't sure she believed him. Trusting men was as foreign to her as owning diamond earrings.

He sat back and wrapped his hands around his mug of coffee. "You should drink your cocoa before it gets cold."

Annie lifted the cup to her lips and took a sip of the rich, sweet chocolate. It helped steady her nerves and gave her a chance to think about what she needed to do next. Shane was making it evident that he wasn't about to go away.

Suspecting he was right about the law, she had no intention of making it a legal matter. Even with the testimony of Marge as her sponsor, Annie doubted that a judge would overlook her past in a custody battle. For the moment, Corporal Shane Ross had the upper hand.

Would he turn out to be a dog in the manger? Once he got what he wanted, would he lose interest? His story about the little boy he had lost to a deadbeat dad didn't mean that he wouldn't follow the same pattern. Perhaps instead of fighting him, she should wait and let time do the work for her. Not many of the men she'd known came through on their promises. Why should she think Shane would be any different?

She couldn't quite silence the small voice in the back of her mind that told her this man *was* different.

"Have you thought about adoption?" he asked after a few minutes.

"I've considered it, but I want to keep my baby." She'd admitted the thought aloud for the first time and it felt right.

"That's good to know. Thank you for telling me."

Had she made a mistake? Confiding in him was easier than she'd expected. She quickly resolved not to give him any more information. "I should be going."

"But you haven't finished your drink."

"I want to leave now."

He looked ready to argue but finally nodded and said, "Sure."

He motioned to the waitress and paid the check. Annie picked up her purse and headed for the door.

Outside, he walked beside her to the staff parking spaces, stopping beside a low-slung red Mustang with a wide black stripe down the hood. The car was obviously not new, but it was in pristine condition. He unlocked and opened the door for her. As she got in, she took note of the difference between his vehicle and hers. His didn't have rips in the fabric of the front seat. His radio had buttons, while hers didn't even have the knobs it had come with. She was pretty sure his heater worked no matter how cold it got. Judging by this, he could afford to pay child support.

Temptation came in many forms. Only knowing that she would have to give up more than she would gain kept her from accepting his previous offer. She and her baby wouldn't have a lavish life, but they would have enough.

"Nice wheels," she said when he slid into the driver's seat.

"Thanks. This is a 1973 Mustang Mach One. This puppy is my pride and joy."

"You can afford a classic car like this on a corporal's salary?"

He laughed. "She wasn't much to look at when I first found her, but it still took two summers of roofing in the hot Texas sun to pay for her back when I was a teenager. Restoring her has been a kind of hobby of mine ever since. Besides, I live on base so I don't have many expenses. This car is my one luxury. Annie, is the fact that I'm in the Army part of the reason you don't want me involved with our baby?"

It was as good a reason as any. "To my mind, guns and babies don't to go together."

"There's a lot more to the Army than guns."

"I'm sure that's true, but how many years have you been in?"

"Six."

"And how many different places have you been stationed in in that time?"

"Including basic training? Four."

"That's not exactly a blueprint for maintaining close family ties."

"No, but it's not impossible if you're willing to work at it." She heard the resignation creeping into his voice, even if he wouldn't admit as much.

She drove home her point. "Tell me how we could make it work. Should we ship the kid back and forth between us every six months? Aren't you going to Germany soon?"

"We live in the same place now."

"But not for long. I might decide I want to move. Who

knows where you'll be stationed after Germany. It's too complicated. I need to get on with my life and you need to get on with yours. I wish now that I hadn't told you."

"No, don't wish that."

A sadness to match his settled over her. "You probably wish you had never met me," she said softly.

He stared at his hands clasped around the top of the steering wheel for a long moment, then looked over and met her gaze. "No, I don't."

He started the engine and shifted into Reverse. She gave him her home address, then leaned back into the plush seat. He didn't speak during the ride and neither did she.

When he pulled up in front of her house, he shut off the engine and turned toward her. "I can't help thinking that one of the reasons you don't want me around the baby is because you don't know me well."

"I know you well enough."

"If you're referring to the night we met, I'll be the first to admit that we started off all wrong."

"So?"

He pressed his hand to his chest, his expression earnest and intense. "I'd like to change that. I'd like to get to know you and I'd like you to get to know me. Someday the kid is going to ask about me. I'd like you to be able to tell him something about what I do and what kind of person I am."

"What are you suggesting? That we start dating?" She didn't bother to hide her sarcasm.

"That's an excellent idea. What are you doing Saturday afternoon?"

Chapter Four

"Annie, you seem awfully quiet tonight. Is something bothering you?" Marge diced another carrot and added it to the large kettle of vegetable soup simmering on the back burner of her stove.

At the long pine table nearby, Annie closed the book she wasn't actually reading. Since she couldn't come to a decision about what to do by herself, perhaps Marge could help. "When Shane Ross brought me home yesterday...he asked me out."

"Like—on a date?" The astonished inquiry came from Marge's thirteen-year-old daughter, Olivia, as she breezed into the kitchen and pulled open the fridge door. With her sleek chin-length dark hair and dark eyes, she and Annie could have passed for sisters.

Marge turned and scowled at her only child. "Get out of the fridge. Supper will be ready in half an hour. And what is so surprising about Annie being asked out on a date?"

Olivia rolled her eyes and took a container of flavored

yogurt before she shut the door. "It's just that she never goes out."

While it was true, it was embarrassing to have a teenager point out her total lack of a social life.

Annie said, "He didn't exactly ask me for a date. He asked me to come and watch his unit perform on base Saturday afternoon. It's some kind of community appreciation day."

"Oh, oh, is he the one with the horses?" Olivia's eyes widened with interest.

"Yes, he's in the mounted color guard. How did you know that?"

"Crystal told me about him. Heather, one of my friends from school, saw them ride last year. She said they were *awesome*. She's going with her family. I heard that there's going to be a carnival and tons of stuff to see and do. I wish we could go. Could we, Mom? Please?"

Marge shook her head. "I'm sorry, sweetie, but I'm working at the clinic on Saturday."

Olivia's excited expression turned to disappointment. She plopped into a chair beside Annie. "You're always working at that clinic."

"Which is exactly why you have a roof over your head and food in the refrigerator, young lady."

"It's not much of a roof. It leaks like a faucet in the corner of my room when it rains."

Annie nudged the pouting girl with her elbow. "Your mom does important work at the mental-health clinic. If she hadn't been there for me, I wouldn't be here today. She saved my life."

"I know, but I'd really like to see the Army's horses."

Leaning forward, Annie winked at the girl. "Plus a few good-looking guys dressed in romantic cavalry uniforms sporting sabers and pistols."

Olivia's frown changed to a conspiratory grin shared between the two of them. "That, too."

After seasoning the pot with salt and pepper, Marge put the lid on and lowered the heat. Wiping her hands on a paper towel, she turned to Annie. "What did you say when Shane invited you?"

"I said I'd think about it."

"And have you?"

Far more than she cared to admit. With his deep-timbred voice and slow Texas drawl, his bright blue eyes and soft, enchanting smile, Shane was almost all she *had* thought about these past few days. Her plan to tell him about her pregnancy and then dismiss him from her life wasn't exactly working out. "I don't think I should go."

"Why not?"

Annie shrugged. "I don't know."

She didn't really have a reason, at least not one she wanted to talk about. She didn't want to go because she suspected that the more she saw of Corporal Ross the harder it would be to ignore his request to be included in her baby's life—*their* baby's life.

"Why don't you go and take Olivia with you? That way you won't have to go by yourself. Plus, Olivia won't have to spend the next two days giving me those deep sighs and pitiful looks that mean I'm the world's worst mother because I'm not letting her do something she wants."

Olivia's face brightened. "Yeah, that would be great! And I don't think you're the world's worst mom."

"That's not what you said when I wouldn't let you get your belly button pierced."

"Mom, that was weeks ago—and so not fair. Heather got hers pierced."

"Just because Heather does something doesn't mean you have to do it, too."

"She's not the only one in my class that has a belly-button ring."

"That still doesn't make it right. Besides, while you're— "

"I know, I know. While I'm living in this house I have to live by your rules."

"That's right, and I'm tough on you because…why?"

"Because you love me and you want me to grow up to be a responsible adult."

"Right!"

Listening to their exchange, Annie wondered if she would be as good a mother as Marge was. In spite of having lost her husband in a car accident when Olivia was a toddler, Marge's faith and courage never seemed to waiver. Making a home for herself and her child must have been hard enough, but somehow Marge found the strength to do more. She had reached out to other young women in need, opening her home to some of them and offering hope and compassion to everyone who came asking for help.

Olivia gave up arguing with her mother and turned to Annie. "Please, can I go with you to the base? I promise not to be a pain. We'll have fun and you can meet some of my friends."

Annie didn't have the heart to say no in the face of Olivia's wide, pleading eyes and excited demeanor. Or maybe she really did want to see Shane again. "Sure, I'll take you."

"Sweet!" Olivia jumped up and threw her arms around Annie's neck. "Thanks. You won't regret it. I'm going to call Heather. We have to decide where to meet."

Scooping up her yogurt and pausing only long enough to pull a spoon out of one of the drawers, Olivia hurried toward the phone in the living room.

Marge drew out a chair and sat down beside Annie. "Maybe I shouldn't have suggested that you take her. Sometimes I let my own guilt about being a poor mother cloud my judgment where Olivia is concerned."

"You aren't a bad mother."

"Perhaps not, but I'm one that doesn't get to spend as much time with my child as I would like. If you decide you don't want to go, I'll make other arrangements for Olivia."

"I won't regret having Olivia's company, but I might regret going at all."

"Why is that?"

"I'm so confused about what I should be doing. When I found out I was pregnant, everything I hoped I could do with my life came to a grinding halt. I agreed to tell Shane about the baby because I honestly thought he wouldn't care. But he does care. At least I think he does. He says he does."

"Do you like Shane?"

Annie took a long time to form her answer. "Maybe, but what's the point?"

Marge tilted her head slightly. "What's the point of exploring your feelings for the father of your child? I think that's pretty obvious. The two of you have a lot to work out."

"Marge, I've never had a relationship with any man that wasn't based on alcohol, including the night I met Shane. By the time I was a junior in high school I was already keeping a bottle stashed under my bed so I had something to help get me started in the mornings. I don't remember half the dates I went on because I got smashed as often and as fast as I could. Once my parents kicked me out, I lived with one guy after another. Some of them, I barely remember their names, but if they were buying me booze…I thought I loved them."

"That isn't your life now."

"No. I've been sober for eighty-eight days, and in that time I haven't so much as looked at another guy. I have no idea how to judge Shane's sincerity or how to act around a man who doesn't have a drink in his hand."

"You told me that Shane wants you to keep the baby and he wants to be involved in the child's life. Do you have a reason to doubt that he's sincere?"

"No, but I can't see what he has to gain by it."

Shaking her head sadly, Marge said, "Not every man commits to a purpose because he has something to gain. Some men commit because it is the right thing to do."

"None of the ones I know."

"Then perhaps you should get to know Shane better. Find out if he is the kind of man you want your child to know."

Sighing, Annie picked up her book and opened it. "Maybe I'm making a bigger deal out of this than I need to. He only asked me to come watch his unit perform. It's not like he asked me to marry him or something."

Why that comment had popped out of her mouth, Annie had no idea. She shot a startled glance at Marge in time to see her hide a smile behind her hand. Sitting up, Annie said, "That didn't mean that I've been thinking about him as husband material."

A quick grin curved Marge's lips, but she pressed them into a firm line. "No, of course it doesn't mean that."

"It doesn't!" Annie shot to her feet. "I'll be outside if you need me."

She stomped out the door, determined not to give Corporal Shane Ross another thought. Her determination lasted only as long as it took her to reach the backyard and look up into the cloudless blue sky.

Shane's eyes were bright blue. What color eyes would the baby have? Annie hoped they would be brown. Otherwise, she would be reminded every day that her child was his child, too.

Shane pulled his saddle cinch tight and checked the grandstands again. The colorful crowd was growing by the minute as the time for his detachment's demonstration neared. Twice he had seen women with long dark braids climbing the steps of the bleachers, but when they'd turned around to take their seats, neither of them had been the woman he was looking for. His faint hope that Annie would come today faded a little more.

"Do you see her?" Avery asked as he finished saddling his mount, Dakota.

Shane resumed checking Jasper's tack. "No, but I'm not surprised. I didn't really think she would show."

Adjusting his flat-topped trooper's hat, Avery said, "If she doesn't, there are plenty of other women out there waiting to be impressed. I'm ready to shock and awe those two blond beauties at this end of the bleachers."

Shaking his head, Shane said, "If you hit even one balloon with your sword, we'll all be shocked."

"Very funny. You know I'm better at sabers than you are."

"I don't know any such thing. You'll be breaking your neck trying to see if the pretty girls are watching, and I'll be cutting down targets. I think I'll hit four for every one that you get."

"Dream on!"

"We shall see."

Smoothing the coat of his dark blue wool 1854-style cavalry uniform, Shane stepped into the stirrup and swung into the saddle. "The crowd is a lot bigger than I was expecting. It's good to see so much support."

Avery spent another few seconds making sure his saddle and girth were secure, then he mounted Dakota. Prancing in eagerness, Dakota sidestepped into Jasper and then let out a loud whinny.

Sudden static filled the air as the loudspeakers on the reviewing stand came on. Avery tapped Shane on the shoulder and pointed to a woman with short auburn hair climbing the steps to the platform. "Hey, it's Sergeant Mandel."

Shane reached over to pat Dakota's neck. "You recognized her, didn't you, fella?"

"Lindsey's not a sergeant anymore," Shane reminded his friend. "She left the service and works in public affairs now."

"She'll always be Sergeant Mandel to me."

"Yeah, I miss her, too."

Until recently, Lindsey had been a member of the Commanding General's Mounted Color Guard, and her brother had once owned Dakota. Lindsey's skills and her dedication to the unit and the Army were something rare. Even after leaving the service, she had found a way to promote public awareness of the many and varied jobs the Army performed.

Lindsey, dressed in a dark blue dress with a red-and-white scarf draped around her neck, leaned close to the microphone. "Ladies and gentlemen, welcome to Fort Riley's Community Appreciation Day. I hope you've been enjoying the festivities so far. I understand the obstacle tent where you get to wear night-vision goggles has been a big hit with the kids."

A dozen isolated shouts of agreement went up from the stands. She smiled in response. "If you were impressed with our latest gadgets, I'm sure you'll be even more impressed with the demonstration you're about to see here."

Music poured out of the loudspeakers around the field, and the muted but stirring strains of the Battle Hymn of the Republic filled the air.

"Long before we had tanks, planes and Black Hawk helicopters, the U.S. Army relied on another method of moving troops quickly into battle. I'm talking about the horse. While mechanization has made the use of the horse obsolete on the battlefield, we here at Fort Riley have not forgotten the contributions the horse soldier has made to our history. Once called the Cradle of the Cavalry, Fort Riley housed the Cavalry Training School until the cavalry was disbanded in 1943."

Captain Watson rode up beside the eight troopers waiting with their horses at one end of the parade ground. "Corporal, form up the detachment."

"Yes, sir." Saluting smartly, Shane called out the order and the men and horses moved into a column of two. Another soldier on the ground handed Shane the unit banner. When the colors were unfurled, he gripped the staff and awaited his orders.

"In 1992," Lindsey continued, "the Commanding General's Mounted Color Guard was reestablished to honor that long tradition. These men train from the same cavalry manual used to train soldiers during the Civil War. This unit serves as ambassadors for the Army, as well as a living history exhibition. It is arduous work, but the level of horsemanship these soldiers attain is nothing short of remarkable. Please give a round of applause to both the men and the horses of our own Commanding General's Mounted Color Guard."

Captain Watson gave the order, and the unit sprang into action.

The crowd cheered wildly as nine matching bay horses galloped across the grassy field with the flag snapping in the wind. For Shane, this was the best part of his job. The chance to reenact this special piece of America's past filled him with pride.

At the opposite end of the field, the column split in two. Both lines turning in unison, the men and their mounts continued at a gallop toward a row of low hurdles along the edges of the parade ground. A dozen red and white balloons decorated each end of the barriers, but by the end of the performance there would only be a few of them left.

When all the hurdles had been cleared, the riders merged into a double row again and came to a halt. Handing the banner to a man on the ground, Shane then drew his saber from its scabbard. He looked over at Avery and nodded. Together they rode back into the jumps. As his horse, Jasper, sailed into the air, Shane slashed the tops of two balloons. Jasper raced on, unfazed by the loud pops. At the second jump, Shane's sword caught two more of the helium-filled targets. From the corner of his eye he saw Avery take out three, and he chuckled to himself. Avery was good, but he often needed a little push to really excel.

When the entire group had completed their run, they reformed into two groups. At a command, they merged and began a mock battle designed to display both their swordsmanship and their mounts' abilities to maneuver at close quarters.

From the bottom row of the bleachers near the reviewing stand Annie listened to the clash of steel against steel as she watched the exhibition with Olivia at her side. A shiver of fear ran down her spine. It would be so easy for one of the men to be hurt. From the sound of it, the swords were heavy—but surely they weren't sharp.

She easily picked Shane out of the group of milling riders. He certainly seemed to be enjoying himself as he and another man traded what looked like serious blows.

On cue, the battling group parted and formed up for another gallop around the grounds. After one circuit, the riders headed into the hurdles again, this time with pistols drawn. The bark of gunfire and the smell of gun smoke filled the air as the men shot the remaining balloons while their mounts sailed through the jumps.

"I told you it would be exciting. Did you see the way their horses didn't even hesitate?" Olivia stood to get a better view.

"Very impressive," Annie admitted, watching Shane complete the course with ease. He looked at home on horseback...and so very handsome in his uniform.

"There you are. I've been looking all over for you."

Annie leaned forward to see a young girl slide into a vacant space on the other side of Olivia. Dressed in a bright red tank top and short cutoff jeans, Olivia's friend appeared several years older than Annie had expected. On closer inspection, she realized the girl's heavy makeup helped disguise her youthful features. Olivia, wearing a blue T-shirt with smooching white puppies on the front, looked much younger and far more innocent.

"You said to meet you by the viewing stand. We've been here for half an hour," Olivia replied.

"Oh, right. Well, I'm here now. Come on, this is boring. Let's go over to the carnival rides."

Glancing between her friend and Annie, Olivia said, "Can I go with Heather?"

Torn between wanting to let Olivia go with her friends and not wanting her out of sight, Annie said, "I thought you wanted to watch the horses."

"I've seen enough."

With one last look at Shane, Annie pulled her purse

strap up on her shoulder. "All right, I guess we can go take in a few rides. But you aren't going to get me on that Ferris wheel."

"You don't have to come," Heather said quickly.

"She's right, Annie. You can stay and watch the rest of this."

"We'll be back in thirty minutes, I promise." Heather's smile was disarming, but still, Annie hesitated.

"We shouldn't split up. This is a pretty big crowd."

"We'll ride a few rides and then come right back."

"If we hurry, we won't have to wait in line," Heather added. "Nearly everyone is here."

Annie glanced toward the midway and noticed that what Heather said was true. The spinning tilt-a-whirl and the Ferris wheel were only half full. Just the sight of the dizzying rides was enough to bring back her morning sickness. Getting on a ride was the last thing she wanted to do.

She studied Olivia's hopeful face. "Half an hour, right?"

Olivia's eyes brightened. "Right. Thanks, Annie. You're the best."

Watching the pair of them hurry away, Annie realized that she didn't feel like "the best." Instead she wondered if she had made a bad decision.

Her uncertainty kept her from enjoying the rest of the demonstration. Shane and his unit's feats of horsemanship barely held her interest. She glanced frequently toward the rides and checked her watch.

Forty minutes later, Shane's exhibition had ended and the stands began to empty. Annie's initial annoyance at being kept waiting rapidly turned to concern. By the time another twenty minutes had gone by only a handful of people remained, and most of them were working their way to the bottom of the bleachers or meeting in small groups at the edge of the field. Her growing concern turned to outright worry.

Where could they be? It wasn't like Olivia to break her word. A dozen unpleasant scenarios darted though Annie's mind, most of them fueled by distasteful memories of her own teenage years. Letting the girls go off alone had been a stupid decision.

As the few remaining onlookers cleared out, Annie climbed to the top of the bleachers hoping to catch a glimpse of the girls coming her way. Searching the growing crowds on the midway proved to be fruitless. She was simply too far away. If she joined the throng and tried to find the girls, she could pass within a dozen yards and not see them.

Wait here or go out to look for them? She wasn't sure what to do.

Checking her watch again, she saw the girls were over an hour late now. She couldn't wait any longer.

Help me find them, Lord. I'm depending on You.

Hurrying back down the steps, Annie stopped short at the sight of Shane standing in a group in front of her. Several of the men in his company were gathered around the female announcer. A blond man leaning on a cane stood beside her. Smiling and joking with his friends, Shane looked like the answer to her prayers.

He happened to glance her way. His welcoming grin quickly faded as she closed the distance between them. He rushed toward her. "Annie, what's wrong? Are you okay?"

She hadn't realized she was reaching out to him until

his hands closed over hers. The comfort of his grip helped slow her racing heart.

"Olivia—my friend's daughter—came with me today, and now I can't find her. She said she'd be back in thirty minutes, but that was more than an hour ago. Something's happened to her. I know it."

Chapter Five

Shane's fear dropped away and relief rushed in when he realized there wasn't anything wrong with Annie. Calming her became his next priority. She was seriously alarmed. That couldn't be good for either her or the baby.

"Take it easy. I'm sure nothing has happened to your friend's daughter. Where did you last see her?"

"She went with another girl to ride the carnival rides."

"Maybe she just forgot the time."

"Maybe, but this isn't like her. Olivia is only thirteen, but she is a responsible kid. She might be ten minutes late but not an hour and ten minutes."

"Okay, we'll help you search for her." He motioned to his friends and they gathered around.

Annie gave a brief description of both girls and what they were wearing. Suddenly her eyes widened as she looked at Shane. "I don't know Heather's last name. I don't know how to contact her family. How could I be so careless?"

Captain Watson quickly took charge. "Avery, take five

men and begin a search at the far end of the old post, working back to here. From horseback you should have an easier time searching the crowds. The rest of the base is closed off, so unless they left by car they'll still be here. I'll notify security to begin checking vehicles leaving the base. Have you called the girl's mother to see if she rode home with someone else?"

"No. Marge is at work. I don't know if I should call and alarm her or give the girls a little more time. I know Olivia wouldn't leave without telling me first. I should be out looking for her."

Shane realized that she was still holding his hand. Her tight grip and the tone of her voice told him how worried she was.

Lindsey stepped forward and said gently, "Why don't you and I wait here in case she comes back."

Shane nodded his thanks. "That's a good idea. Annie, this is Lindsey Mandel. She's a close friend of mine. And this is her fiancé, Dr. Brian Cutter. Lindsey can wait here with you while we go and look for her."

Annie turned to Shane. "I can't sit around any longer. I have to go look for her."

Somehow he knew not to argue with her. Maybe it was the determined look in her eyes or maybe it was knowing she didn't give in easily when she had made up her mind. "Okay, Lindsey and Brian will wait here in case she comes back. I'll come with you."

"Thank you." She drew a deep breath and gave his hand a squeeze before she released it.

"Let's start with the midway," he suggested.

She nodded in agreement and hurried away. He caught

up to her in several strides. Side by side they made their way through the array of food vendors and military equipment. Shane searched the crowds for a glimpse of a girl in a blue shirt with kissing puppies on the front. Suddenly Annie darted away from his side toward a group of teenagers wearing Kevlar vests and helmets who were taking turns shooting paintballs from realistic-looking rifles.

Annie grabbed Olivia by the shoulder and spun her around, prepared to give the girl the scolding she deserved. In the next second she realized it wasn't Olivia but another girl with the same shirt who was staring at her in stunned surprise.

"I'm sorry," Annie mumbled. "I thought you were someone else."

Turning away, she surveyed the crowd again. Where could Olivia be? Pressing a hand to her forehead, she tried to imagine what she was going to tell Marge. Her friend had entrusted her with her daughter's safekeeping, and Annie had let her down.

If she couldn't keep an eye on one child for the afternoon, what on earth was she doing thinking about raising one of her own?

One of Shane's men came riding up. Stepping to his side, Shane asked, "Any luck?"

"Not yet. You?"

"Nothing. Where haven't we looked?"

"We've covered the midway, the Red Cross tent, the shooting range and the grandstands. I don't know where else to look."

Annie bit her lower lip. "Has anyone checked the carnival workers' trailers?"

The rider shook his head. Shane said, "You start at the north end, we'll start over here."

With Shane close behind her, Annie headed between the red-striped tent of the snow-cone vendor and a small yellow trailer offering corn dogs and hamburgers for sale. The area immediately behind the midway was a jumble of stakes and ropes and electric cords running from loud, smelly diesel generators. Beside a long truck painted with the amusement company's logo and pictures of the different rides, Annie came to an abrupt halt.

Heather sat at a picnic table, laughing with two young men dressed in greasy white shirts and stained jeans. Olivia sat slumped at the table beside her. Empty beer bottles littered the ground around them.

Relief made Annie's knees weak. She drew a quick breath and said, "That's her."

With the next breath Annie's anger spiked and she stormed toward the errant pair. "Olivia Lilly, what do you think you are doing?"

Heather made a quick attempt to hide the bottle she held behind her back. "Ms. Delmar. I'm sorry, I guess we forgot about the time."

"I guess you did," Shane growled. "Annie has been out of her mind with worry. We've got half the base looking for you. Where are your parents?"

"They went home."

"They went home and left you here by yourself?"

"I told them I'd catch a ride with Olivia."

The young men with her took one look at Shane's scowl and suddenly found things to do elsewhere.

Olivia raised her head off the table and gave a vague smile. "Is it time to go?"

"It is way past time," Annie replied, pulling the girl to her feet.

Olivia swayed for a moment, then sat abruptly. "Oops."

"I can't believe this. After everything your mother has taught you about making good choices, this is what you do when her back is turned?"

"It's not her fault," Heather offered. "She just wanted to taste a beer."

Annie snatched the bottle from Heather's hand and tossed it in a nearby trash can. "I'm sure you can share the blame equally. As will the young men who were here. I want their names."

Knowing that her own life had spiraled out of control when she was only a few years older than Olivia made Annie's blood run cold. This never would have happened if she had taken her responsibilities more seriously. She was as much to blame as anyone.

Shane laid a hand on her shoulder. "I'll let the others know we've located her so they can call off the search. Wait here until I get back and I'll see that you get home."

Annie tried her best to smile. "Thank you for your help, Shane, but I can manage now."

"I'll be back anyway." He turned and jogged back the way they had come.

"I think I'm going to be sick." White-faced, Olivia pressed a hand to her mouth. A second later she was.

As Annie attended to her, she couldn't help but pray that

this would turn out to be a lesson Olivia wouldn't soon forget.

Later, as Shane helped Annie settle the teary-eyed girl in the backseat of her car, she tried again to thank him. He waved aside her expression of gratitude. "This isn't your fault."

"I don't see it that way—and I'm afraid Olivia's mother won't see it that way, either. She was very upset when I called her and told her what had happened. Did you locate Heather's family?"

"Yes. Her dad picked her up at the security booth a few minutes ago."

"Was he angry?"

"I think he was more upset by having to make a trip back here than he was about her drinking. He said, 'Kids experiment,' like that explained his underage daughter getting one of her friends drunk. He'd better rein her in now or he's really going to have a problem child on his hands."

A problem child. How many times had she heard that label from her family? Crossing her arms over her chest, she leaned against the car door and stared at the ground. "I was a problem child."

"Were you?"

She slanted a look at him, wanting to see his reaction. For some reason, it mattered. "Yes. When I wasn't much older than Olivia."

He settled one hip against the hood of the car beside her. "Why was that?"

"I wasn't a happy kid. I never felt like I fit in until I started drinking. I wish I could say I had a reason for my alcoholism, but the truth is I didn't. Unlike a lot of alcoholics, I wasn't abused or mistreated. Drinking was socially acceptable in my family, but I couldn't stop there. It became all I wanted, and I did anything I could to feed my habit. I lied, I cheated, I stole."

"What changed?"

"At first, nothing. My parents tried everything, but in the end they were forced to sever our relationship. I don't blame them. I wrecked their lives."

"I find that hard to believe."

"It took a long time for me to see the light. You have no idea of the harm I caused."

"No one leads a blameless life."

"True. We are all sinners. That's what makes God's love for us so very special."

"I don't know about that."

"Do you believe?"

"In God? Sure. Am I a churchgoer? No."

Annie turned and pulled open her car door. "I'm sorry to hear that. Of all the things our baby is going to need in his or her life, people who have strong faith tops the list."

As Shane watched Annie drive away, he allowed himself a small smile. She had said "our baby." It wasn't much, but it was a beginning. Now if he only had some idea how to make the next move. He needed help.

Leaving the makeshift parking lot that had been cordoned off on a grassy field for the festivities that day, he walked along the tree-lined streets of the old post. Large limestone buildings and Victorian-style houses sat back from the now-quiet streets. The white stone walls had mellowed over the decades to a pale yellow that gave this part of the post a special warmth and steeped it in nostalgia.

Clusters of lilacs in the yards beside the wraparound porches of several turn-of-the-century houses lent their sweet, coy fragrance to the late-afternoon air.

Following the twisting maze of roads and walkways, he eventually found himself outside the building that housed the post's public affairs department. He climbed a set of wooden steps and opened the door to a small reception room on the second story. It was empty. Down a short hallway he found an open office door. Lindsey Mandel sat at her desk, looking tired.

She glanced up at the sound of his knock on her doorjamb. "Shane, come in. I heard both missing girls have been found."

He nodded and took a seat in the chair in front of her desk. "All's well that ends well."

"Thank the good Lord for that. I'm certainly glad I didn't have to issue a press release about an Amber Alert. What can I do for you?"

"You met Annie Delmar today. What did you think of her?"

Lindsey leaned back in her chair. "I thought she seemed like an understandably worried woman at the time. Why do you ask?"

What he was about to tell Lindsey didn't reflect well on his own character, but he valued her insight into people—and besides, she was a woman. "Annie is pregnant with my baby."

Lindsey's eyebrows shot up. "Oh! That's a bit of a shock. I didn't know you were seeing anyone. The

CGMCG is a small unit, and that kind of information generally travels fast."

She sat forward, propping her arms on the desk. "I guess congratulations are in order."

"Not really. Annie doesn't want me involved in any way, shape or form."

"I'm sorry your relationship with her didn't work out. That must be hard on both of you."

"That's kind of the thing. We never actually had a relationship. We had one night."

"I see." While her tone didn't convey outright disapproval, it came close.

"I'm telling you this because I need help."

Clearly puzzled, she asked, "Help with what?"

"I need to convince Annie that I deserve to be included in our child's life. I need to know how she thinks so I can come up with a way to sway her."

"In case you missed it, Shane, I don't have children. My wedding isn't until June. I have no idea what it takes to change a pregnant woman's mind."

"I understand that, but take pregnant out of the equation. You're a woman."

"Thank you for noticing."

"You know what I mean. You understand how a woman's mind works. How can I get Annie to trust me enough to include me? I need a plan."

"Spoken like a true military man. Shane, matters of the heart rarely, if ever, follow a plan. Do you love this woman?"

He squirmed in his seat as he tried to put his feelings for Annie into words. "I like her. A lot. There's…I don't know…something special about her. But I need to be involved with my son or daughter. I'm not willing to walk away from that."

"Then my advice would be to stop focusing on the kind of relationship you want with the child and start focusing on the kind of relationship you want with Annie. Women will do almost anything to protect their children. If she sees you as a threat, you'll never earn her trust. Respect is the key."

"How do I make her understand that?"

Lindsey shook her head. "I'm not talking about her. I'm taking about you."

He scowled. "I respect women."

"You're thinking in general terms. Chivalry is fine, but true respect for another human being only comes from knowing them—and it comes from the heart."

Respect from the heart. He nodded. "I understand what you're telling me, but how do Annie and I get past the botched start we made?"

"Baby steps, Shane. Slow, careful baby steps."

Marge stood waiting for them on the front porch when they reached home. The look of disappointment in her eyes as she listened to her daughter's halting and slightly slurred confession was painful for Annie to see.

"Annie, will you excuse us?" Marge asked.

"Of course."

"Olivia, I want to speak to you in private."

Nodding, the girl walked with leaden feet through the doorway. Marge followed her daughter into the house and upstairs to the girl's bedroom.

Annie knew exactly how Olivia was feeling. She took a seat on the beige sofa covered with colorful throw pillows and waited with her gaze riveted to the staircase leading to the upper level. When Marge was done with Olivia, it would undoubtedly be Annie's turn to face the music. She didn't relish the idea.

Would Marge ask her to leave? The prospect was frightening. She didn't have enough money saved to get a place of her own. Without Marge's continued support and counsel, Annie couldn't help wondering if the urge to drink again would overwhelm her the way it had during her last setback.

After thirty long minutes the sound of a door opening and closing upstairs made Annie sit up straight. Only a few months ago she would have taken off rather than apologize and accept responsibility for her actions. Part of her wished she still could, but a deeper part of her was grateful that her newfound faith in God's love kept her from running away.

Marge entered the room and sank onto one of the green recliners flanking the large picture window. Pulling a green-and-gold throw pillow into her lap, Annie buried her fingers in the long fringe to keep her hands from shaking. "I'm so sorry, Marge. I should never have let her go off by herself. This was all my fault."

"Don't be so hard on yourself. Olivia knows right from wrong. I can't believe I didn't see this coming. How can I profess to counsel people for a living when my own daughter can pull a stunt like this?"

"Now who is being hard on themselves?"

Marge managed a weak smile. "You're right. I can only

pray that she learned some kind of lesson from this. How many times can you tell a child that their actions can have serious consequences?"

"If you think it would help, I can talk to her about exactly what those consequences are."

"Thank you. For tonight, I think the headache and sick stomach is enough to stop her from trying this again anytime soon. I hope it is. Can I ask you a question?"

"Sure."

"How young were you when you started drinking?"

"Fifteen."

"How did you get alcohol at that age?"

Looking back, Annie couldn't believe how easy it had been. "My parents had it in the house all the time. They were 'social drinkers.'" She made quote marks with her fingers.

"I'm supposed to be the professional here, but the truth is I'm an angry, scared mother. What should I do?"

"Don't panic."

"That's easy to say." Marge raked a hand through her hair.

Annie sat forward. "Just keep talking to her. Pay attention to how she acts. Search her room if you suspect something. She'll hate you for it, but you can't let that stop you. Alcohol makes people great liars. If she says she's going to stay over at a friend's house, call and check up on her."

"In other words, don't trust my own daughter?"

"My mother trusted me. Maybe if she had been less trusting, things might have turned out differently. I'm not saying it was her fault—it wasn't. I'm saying I got away with it for a long time before anyone noticed. There is no easy answer. You're a good mother, Marge. You'll figure it out."

"I pray with all my heart that you're right." Marge pushed up out of her chair. "I wish my Ben was still here. Raising a child alone is no easy task."

As Marge left the room, Annie laid her head back against the sofa cushion and sighed. She knew raising a child alone wouldn't be easy. Olivia's stunt today had driven home that point and proven once again that Annie had trouble making good choices.

If someone as wise and full of faith as Marge struggles with being a single parent, what chance is there that I can do it by myself?

Yet raising her baby alone was her only option... wasn't it?

Chapter Six

The following Monday afternoon Annie finished cleaning her last room in the east wing of the hotel, happily pocketed a handsome tip and began pushing her cart toward the maids' closet. As she turned into the service corridor, she saw Crystal hurrying toward her. "Annie, you've got to come to the break room."

"In a minute. I need to get restocked first and empty my trash."

Crystal grabbed her arm. "Leave it. You've got to come see this."

"See what?"

"Come on. Quit stalling."

Apparently Crystal wasn't going to take no for an answer. Annie gave in and allowed her friend to pull her toward the break room. Yanking open the door, Crystal grinned and announced, "They're for you!"

Puzzled, Annie glanced from her friend to the group of maids lined up in front of a table. At the sight of Annie, they stepped aside. In the center of the table a large bouquet of sunflowers and green, lacy ferns filled a silver vase to overflowing.

Annie looked from her smiling coworkers to Crystal. "For me? There must be some mistake."

Crystal rushed past her. "There's no mistake. It's got your name on the card. I'm so jealous. Nobody has ever sent me flowers."

No one had ever sent Annie flowers, either. She crossed the room slowly. With hesitant fingers, she touched the velvetlike yellow petals. "Who would send me flowers?"

Marge was the only person Annie could think of who might do something like this, but it wasn't Annie's birthday or any special occasion that she could think of.

Crystal pushed her closer to the table. "Open the card and find out, silly."

Annie stuck her hands in the pockets of her uniform. What if it was some kind of mistake? If she opened the card and found out these weren't for her, she might actually cry. She looked at Crystal. "You open it."

Crystal pulled the card from its plastic holder and held it toward Annie. "I'm not going to read your love note."

Annie snatched it from her hand. "It isn't a love note."

"You don't know that."

After a half second of hesitation, Annie slipped her finger beneath the flap of the envelope. Ripping it open, she pulled out the card. Turning her back on Crystal's interested gaze, she read the brief note handwritten in bold, dark strokes.

I'm sorry you had such a fright on Saturday. I hope you and your friends are all doing okay. Shane

It certainly wasn't a love letter, but it did prove the

flowers were for her. The thoughtfulness of his gesture touched her deeply. She *had* been frightened and worried out of her mind.

"Well, what does it say? Who are they from?" Crystal tried peering over Annie's shoulder.

Tucking the card in her pocket, Annie said, "They're from Shane."

"That is *so* sweet."

"Yes, it is."

"Are you sure you want to get rid of the guy?"

That very question had been buzzing around in the back of Annie's mind since Shane had so willingly offered his help to find Olivia. He wasn't behaving like most of the men she knew. Maybe she had been too quick to dismiss him as another in a long list of mistakes in her life.

She stared at the bouquet, noticing the tiny white flowers tucked in among the greenery. They were baby's breath. Had he asked for them or had it simply been the florist's choice? It was another question that would remain unanswered in the back of her head.

Excluding Shane wasn't an error in judgment. Even if she wanted her baby to know his father, Shane was shipping out to Europe in a few months. One stable, caring parent would be enough for this child. Yet even as the thought ran through Annie's mind, it was quickly followed by the one doubt that never quite faded.

What if she couldn't stay sober? What kind of mother would she be then?

When the doorbell rang the following evening, Annie wasn't surprised to see Shane standing on Marge's front porch. She had been expecting him ever since she had received the flowers. What did catch her unawares was the little skip her heart took at the sight of him. Surely it wasn't because she was happy to see him again. After spending so much time and energy trying to convince him to forget about her and the baby, she should have been angry that he kept showing up. Only…she wasn't.

Dressed in his formal military uniform, he looked even more handsome than he had in his cavalry outfit. For a moment she considered not opening the door, but she realized that was the coward's way out. She needed to show him that a bouquet of flowers, no matter how pretty, wouldn't change her mind about what was best for her baby. Taking a firm grasp on the knob and struggling to compose herself, she opened the door. "What do you want?"

Looking taken aback, he said, "Hello, to you, too."

Annoyed at her lack of composure, she struggled to hide the effect he had on her nerves with bluster. "I'm sorry. Hello, Shane. Now what do you want?"

"Is Olivia home?"

It was Annie's turn to feel taken aback. "Yes."

"May I speak with her?"

She couldn't think of a reason to deny his request. "I guess."

He waited a moment longer. "May I come in or would you rather I wait out here?"

Giving herself a mental shake, Annie stepped back. "Come in. I'll tell Olivia that you're here."

"Thank you."

As he walked in, she couldn't help but notice how large he seemed in their small entryway. The spicy scent of his cologne filled the foyer, and the close quarters left her feeling breathless. She gestured toward the living room through the archway to the right. "Have a seat and I'll tell Marge and Olivia that you're here."

He started into the room, then turned back to smile at her. "I see you got my flowers."

The arrangement sat in the middle of the coffee table in front of the sofa. For an instant Annie wished she had left them in her room, but the bright flowers were simply too pretty not to share with the other women in the house.

"Yes. Thank you. It was a kind thought."

"Don't mention it. How are you feeling, by the way?"

"Fine."

"No ill effects from your scare?"

"None."

"I'm glad. You certainly look well—and very pretty, I might add."

Annie rubbed her palms together and took a step toward the kitchen. "Marge and Olivia are in the backyard. Have a seat and I'll get them."

Turning, she hurried out of the room. The man made her as nervous as a cat in a room full of rocking chairs.

At the back stoop, she saw Olivia unenthusiastically raking grass clippings and depositing them in the trash can. While she hadn't outwardly complained about being grounded, it was plain that she would rather be elsewhere. Marge was pruning the shoulder-high hedge that separated their small yard from the property behind them.

The scent of freshly mown grass and cut cedar mingled with the aroma of someone barbecuing up the block. The sun disappeared behind a mass of dark clouds off to the west, and a cool breeze sprang up to cool Annie's warm cheeks, but the sight of storm clouds piling up in the west only served to increase her nervous tension. Storms terrified her. She quickly crossed the lawn and stopped beside Marge.

"Shane Ross is here and he'd like to speak to you."

Pushing her hair out of her face with the back of one gloved hand, Marge frowned. "He wants to see me?"

"Yes. You and Olivia."

"Me?" Olivia's eyes widened in concern as she propped her rake against the red picnic table that sat in the shade of the yard's ancient maple tree.

Marge scowled at her daughter as she walked past the table and laid her clippers on the corner. "You keep working. I'll see what he wants."

Crossing her arms over her chest, Annie waited anxiously for Marge to return. Away from Shane's overpowering presence, Annie's mind started working again, and she tried to figure out why he had come. When she first saw him at the door, she had assumed he had come to see her— to take up where he had left off trying to convince her that he had as much right as she did to be involved in her baby's future. But he hadn't so much as mentioned the baby except in a roundabout way when he'd asked how she was feeling. So why had he asked to see Marge and Olivia? What was he up to?

She glanced toward the clouds as she rubbed her hands up and down her arms. Were they moving this way?

"I wonder what he wants. Do you think I'm in trouble with the Army?" Making only a halfhearted attempt to continue raking, Olivia's eyes were glued to the back door.

Annie shook her head. "I don't think so."

Olivia frowned at her. "How can you be so sure?"

"Because if you were, they would send someone with a higher rank than a corporal to talk to your mother."

"You mean, like a general?"

"I think a sergeant at the very least."

"I'd really hate to be thrown in the brig."

Annie kept the smile off her face with difficulty. "I might be wrong, but I think you actually have to be *in* the Army to spend time in the brig."

"Oh, well, that's a relief."

The back door opened and Marge emerged from the house with Shane close behind her. They crossed to where Annie and Olivia stood. Marge said, "Olivia, this is Corporal Ross."

"I remember you—sort of."

"You weren't feeling your best when we last met. With your mother's permission, I have a few questions I'd like to ask you." The gentleness of his smile made Annie wish he were looking at her.

Marge said, "We'll be in the house if you need us."

He nodded once. "Thank you, ma'am."

Taking Annie by the elbow, Marge steered her toward the back door. Once they were inside, Marge went to the kitchen sink. Annie joined her, pulling the blue-checkered curtain aside so that she had a view of the pair taking a seat at the picnic table. Marge began to wash her hands. The fragrance of lemon soap vied with smell of ham baking in the oven.

Annie couldn't contain her curiosity any longer. "What does he want?"

"He wants to ask Olivia about the boys who supplied the alcohol. The Army is looking into the incident. They recognize that underage drinking is a very serious problem in the community and they want to help. The military police are questioning Heather. Shane offered to come here because he felt Olivia might feel less threatened by a friend of yours."

"He's not exactly my friend."

Marge pulled a sheet of paper towel from the holder under the cabinet and dried her hands. Turning to face Annie, she said, "He wants to be."

Looking away, Annie chose to ignore the remark. "I hope she tells him what she knows."

"I hope so, too. She didn't want to tell me anything that would get Heather in more trouble, but perhaps she won't feel the same misguided loyalty toward those young men. Tell me— why don't you believe that Corporal Ross wants to be your friend?"

Startled, Annie frowned at her. "I didn't say that."

"Not in so many words, perhaps, but the look on your face plainly says you don't believe he does."

"Do you think he does?"

"I think it's worth taking the chance to find out."

Annie focused her attention out the window. Shane had risen to his feet. He offered his hand to Olivia. She stood and shook it, looking almost grown-up and shyly proud. Dropping the curtain so Shane wouldn't see her spying on him, Annie moved away from the window. When the pair came into the kitchen, she busied herself pulling a stack of plates from the cupboard. She chanced a peek at him. He grinned and winked at her, then spoke to Marge.

"Thank you for letting me speak with Olivia. She's been very helpful."

Marge smiled at her daughter. "I'm glad. Have you had dinner, Corporal?"

"Please call me Shane. No, I haven't eaten." He glanced at his watch. "I'll pick something up on the way back to the base."

"Why don't you join us? We have plenty."

Annie spoke up quickly. "I'm sure that the corporal has to get back to his duties."

"Actually, I'm done for the day. Whatever you're having smells good. If you're certain it won't be a problem, I'd be happy to stay."

"Wonderful. Pull up a chair and join us. It isn't fancy, but it's filling. Olivia, would you please tell Crystal that dinner is ready. Annie, could you set another place for Shane? I'll be back in a minute. I need to put my tools away. They're forecasting rain tonight."

Annie's apprehension about the approaching weather jumped a notch. "Are they calling for severe weather?"

Marge patted Annie's arm. "No, dear. Just a few showers. Are you okay?"

Nodding, Annie turned back to the cupboard. The sound of the back door closing told her Marge had left the room.

"Not scared of a little thunder, are you?" Shane asked, his amusement plain.

Annie bit her tongue to keep from making a rude reply. He probably wasn't scared of anything. It must be nice.

She didn't want him here, but this was Marge's home and Marge had invited him to dinner. Pulling a plate from the shelf, Annie spun around, determined to make the best of it.

"Can I do anything to help?" he offered.

"Leaving would be good."

"Besides disappearing forever through a crack in the floor, is there anything else I can do?"

"That's all I had in mind."

"Sorry. Army regulations strictly forbid military personnel from melting." The hint of humor in his tone had her struggling to hide a smile.

"The front door would work just as well."

"Ah, but then Marge would think that you ran me off."

He was right, but she hated to admit it. She moved past him, being careful not to touch him, and plunked the extra dish on the table.

"Annie, I will leave if my being here upsets you."

"I'm not upset," she countered quickly. *Lord, please forgive that little white lie.*

"Good, because I haven't had a home-cooked meal in ages. Mess hall food is…mess hall food, and something in this kitchen smells great."

"Marge is a good cook." Turning the subject of the conversation to her friend seemed like a safe move.

He leaned a hip against the counter. "She comes across as a very caring person. How long have you known her?"

"Almost two years." She pulled out the flatware they would need from the drawer at the end of the counter and carried the pieces to the table.

"How did you meet?"

"Marge was assigned as my caseworker when I was brought into the emergency room one night."

Annie didn't tell him that it had been the night she had tried to kill herself. Thankfully most of those terrible hours were nothing but a black hole in her memory.

The door to the kitchen opened and Crystal came in, followed by Olivia.

Shane could have growled aloud with frustration. He wanted time alone with Annie. Time to get to know her and for her to get to know him. While he sensed her reluctance to talk to him, as least she hadn't made an excuse to leave the room. It was a small victory but one he would have to be satisfied with for now.

The outside door opened and Marge came in. "I'll just wash up and then we can get started. Sit anywhere you like, Shane. We're not much for ceremony here."

Olivia sat and patted the seat next to her. "Sit here, Shane."

Smiling at her, he took the chair she indicated, but it was Annie he followed with his eyes as she moved around the kitchen, getting the food on the table and filling everyone's glasses with water. When it came to his glass, she leaned in to pick it up and her arm brushed against his shoulder. The sound of her quick indrawn breath sent a jolt of awareness straight through him. Her hands trembled ever so slightly and she sloshed some of the liquid onto the table-top.

"I'm sorry." She had to lean in farther as she mopped up the spill with his paper napkin.

"I'll get it." He took the soggy mess from her and finished the task, half afraid she'd pour the rest of the ice water in his lap if he didn't let her escape.

Crystal made a beeline for the chair across from him. "Hi, there. I'm so glad you could join us, Corporal Ross. I've just been dying to tell you how beautiful I thought your flowers were. I sure wish someone would send me something like that. I'd be forever grateful."

He took note of her come-hither glance. The realization that it didn't interest him as much as catching Annie's downcast gaze came as no surprise. Annie was special in a way he couldn't quite put his finger on. He wanted to spend time with Annie. He wanted to get to know her.

His pending reassignment overseas loomed like the approaching storm clouds outside that were fast blocking the afternoon sunlight. Faced with Annie's reluctance to admit him into her life and the limited amount of time he had to change her mind, he didn't see a way to accomplish that goal.

Marge, at the head of the table, held her hands out to Olivia and Annie seated on either side of her. "Let us give thanks and ask the Lord's blessing on this family and the company gathered here."

Shane met Annie's eyes as she glanced in his direction. The longing in her expression stunned him. Before he could be certain of what he'd seen, she looked away again.

Olivia took her mother's hand and then reached for Shane's. Feeling a bit awkward, he grasped it. Crystal's smile widened as she stretched her arm across the table toward him. He hesitated only a second before clasping her hand. She squeezed his fingers and cast a sidelong glance at Annie before bowing her head.

Marge closed her eyes and said, "We give You thanks, Lord Jesus, for the bounty You have bestowed upon us. Let us be ever mindful that our true strength comes through You. Bless the people gathered here and grant that through Your intercession we may come to grow in love, faith and wisdom. Amen."

"Amen," Shane added to chorus of voices around him. If he couldn't convince Annie of the wisdom of accepting his help, he certainly wasn't above asking God to give him a hand.

"How long have you been in the Army, Shane?" Marge asked as she passed the platter of meat to Olivia.

"Six years now."

"Are you making it your career?"

"Yes, ma'am. The pay isn't great, but it offers me the chance to serve my country, to travel and to learn new things. I can honestly say if it hadn't been for the Army, I never would have learned to shoe a horse."

"Your performance was so cool, wasn't it, Annie?" Olivia slid a thick slice of ham onto her plate and passed the dish to him.

"You mean, the part of it you actually saw?" Marge asked, giving her daughter a disapproving stare.

"Yeah. I wish I had stayed to see all of it," Olivia replied, clearly chastised.

"Maybe you'll get another chance to see us in action." He took a piece of meat and handed the platter to Marge.

Olivia gave him a half smile. "I kinda doubt it."

Marge's stern features relaxed. "I would be interested in seeing your unit in action someday."

Olivia's eyes brightened as she looked at her mother. "Like, after I'm not grounded anymore?"

"Yes, like then."

Crystal leaned toward Shane. "Do you give special tours of the stable?"

"Tours can be arranged through the Department of Public Affairs. The captain assigns the personnel for each tour."

"So it might not be you?"

"Not usually. I have other duties." He forked a piece of meat into his mouth.

"Oh." Clearly disappointed, Crystal turned her attention back to her meal.

"This ham is great," he said. Hoping to draw Annie out, he asked, "Do you like to cook?"

Olivia and Crystal both burst out laughing. Annie stared at her plate.

"Annie can't boil water," Crystal said. "Never let her cook you a meal."

"Annie is learning," Marge said. "Cooking is a skill that takes practice, like everything else."

"She makes an okay tuna casserole," Olivia added as if trying to make up for her unkindness.

The sound of thunder suddenly rumbled through the house. Annie flinched and grew pale. "It's storming."

Marge laid a hand on her arm. "It's just a shower. It will be over soon."

"Please excuse me." Laying her napkin on the table, Annie hurried from the room.

Shane looked to Marge for an explanation. Smiling sadly, she said, "Annie is deathly afraid of storms."

He could have kicked himself for teasing her earlier, but how could he have known? Still, it must have made him look like a first-class jerk in her eyes.

"What made her scared of them?" he asked.

"I'm not even sure she knows."

Olivia tossed her napkin on the table. "May I be excused also?"

"Are you scared of thunder, too?" he asked, glancing at the others in the room.

"No, but when it rains, the roof leaks in my room. I need to put a pail under the spot before my floor gets wet again."

"Of course, dear. Would you check on Annie before you come back?"

"Not a problem."

"Thanks, honey. The pail is under the sink in the bathroom."

Crystal rose, too. "I noticed a spot on the ceiling in the laundry room after the last storm. Maybe I should get a pail, too, just in case."

Shane frowned at Marge. "If your roof is leaking that badly, you should see about getting it fixed before you have serious damage."

"I know. Getting the roof repaired is on my to-do list. While the shingles themselves may actually fit into my budget, the cost of a roofing contractor won't. They're expensive."

"I worked as a roofer when I was a teenager. My foster father was a contractor and he taught me a lot about the business. I'd be happy to take a look and see exactly what you need."

"I couldn't ask you to do that."

"You didn't ask. I offered. It could be that you only have a few shingles missing and you don't need a whole new roof."

"Wouldn't that be wonderful? If you're sure, please take a look. I'll get you a ladder."

"After the rain stops."

Grinning, she nodded. "Of course. After the rain. In the meantime, would you like some dessert? I picked up a sinfully delicious lemon pound cake from the bakery today."

As Marge served him a generous slice of cake, Olivia and Crystal rejoined them, but Annie remained absent. Outside, the summer storm produced a brief, generous downpour as it passed overhead, but it soon moved off into the distance and the sound of thunder faded away.

He glanced frequently toward the door to the other room, but Annie didn't return. Perhaps she had found a way to avoid him after all.

Chapter Seven

Annie chanced a peek out the door of her room when she heard the front door open and close downstairs. A few seconds later she heard the sound of someone climbing the stairs. When Olivia came into sight, Annie opened the door wider. "Is he gone?"

"You are such a chicken."

"I can't help it that storms petrify me."

"I wasn't talking about the weather."

"I know, but is he gone?"

"I think so. He and Mom walked out together."

Annie wanted to be relieved, but instead she realized what she felt was disappointment. How silly was that?

A loud thunk sounded against the outside of the house. She and Olivia stared at each other for a moment. Wide-eyed, Olivia whispered, "What was that?"

"I don't know."

They both hurried to the window in Annie's room. The top rungs of a ladder protruded above the roof of the back porch. As they stared, Shane's head appeared above the edge.

Annie did a double take. "What is he doing?"

"Beats me. Hey, are you two eloping? That is so romantic. It's just like Romeo and Juliet."

"Don't be an idiot. I have no intention of eloping with the man."

"Then why is he on a ladder outside your bedroom window?"

"How should I know?" Annie jerked up the sash. "Shane, what do you think you're doing?"

He had taken off his jacket and tie and discarded them before his climb. The sleeves of his white shirt were rolled up and displayed brown, muscular forearms. Stepping gingerly off the ladder, he looked up and located her in the window.

"Are you okay? When you didn't come back to finish dinner, I was worried about you."

"So you climbed onto the roof to look for me?"

"Marge asked me to take a look at the shingles and see how much work needs to be done. Just from here I can see that she is going to need a whole new roof on this porch. Excuse me."

He walked up to the low edge of the eaves beside her window and hoisted himself up and out of sight. Leaning out the window, she twisted around to stare at the spot where he had vanished. The sound of scrambling feet overhead made her call out, "Be careful up there."

His face reappeared above her. "Worried about me?" He sounded almost hopeful.

"No."

His smile widened into a cocky grin. "Yes, you are. Admit it."

"I am not." Pulling her head back in, she slammed down the window hard enough to rattle the glass, but it didn't completely block the sound of his hearty laughter.

"I have no idea what I thought I saw in him."

Olivia leaned against the dresser. Crossing her arms over her chest, she regarded Annie with one eyebrow raised. "Are you kidding? He's a hunk."

"A lot of men are cute. That doesn't mean anything."

"He's a hunk and he's really nice. I was scared silly when he asked to speak to me earlier. I thought I was in for another scolding. But he talked to me like I was a grown-up. I didn't want to rat on Heather and the boys who got us the beer, but Shane made me see that I wasn't helping them by keeping quiet."

"He did?"

"Yeah. Why are you so dead set against liking him?"

Why was she? He'd shown nothing but kindness and concern for her since the day she told him about the baby. If she hadn't known that men were users, she might have been tempted to accept his offer of assistance. Shaking her head, she said, "It's complicated."

Rolling her eyes, Olivia uncrossed her arms and headed for the door. "Adults always say that when they don't know the answer to the question."

Out of the mouths of babes, Annie thought as Olivia closed the door behind her. She didn't know why she couldn't accept Shane's offer of friendship. Distrust was an old habit that was hard to break.

Like drinking.

Footsteps overhead made her look up. Giving her life over to God had been her salvation from alcohol. What if God had brought Shane into her life for a reason? But for *what* reason? To show her how weak she still was? If meeting Shane had been some kind of test, Annie knew she had failed miserably.

The sounds of scraping and scrambling gave way to the sound of a heavy object sliding down the roof, then the muffled thud of something hitting the ground. Annie dashed to the window and jerked it open with her heart lodged in her throat.

"Shane, are you okay?"

Had he fallen? The front side of the house didn't have a porch like the one below her window. It was a straight two-story drop to the concrete drive. Could he survive it? She closed her eyes and prayed.

Please, God, don't let anything bad happen to him.

"Sorry if I scared you." She opened her eyes to see a pair of black boots dangling from the eaves overhead. A second later he jumped down and landed in front of her. His wide grin turned her fear to annoyance.

"What was that?" she demanded.

"Just a limb that had blown down in the storm. It was wedged against the chimney. After I fix this roof, I'll cut those trees back a little. A limb that size could break a shingle or two, and Marge would be right back where she started with the rain pouring in."

"We don't need you to fix the roof."

"Someone needs to do it and I don't mind this kind of work. A few hours each evening and I can have it done in a couple of weeks." He walked over to the ladder.

"You have a job," she called.

Stepping onto the ladder, he gave her a short salute. "The Army is more than a job. It's an adventure."

He vanished from sight before she could think of a comeback. She sat on the windowsill in disbelief. Shane would be here! He would be working where she lived. Possibly for several weeks! The only way she would be able to avoid him would be to lock herself in her room or stop coming home. Why on earth would Marge agree to such a thing? She had to know what an uncomfortable position it put her in.

The answer was obvious: Marge liked Shane. While Annie's instincts might be biased against men, Marge had no such problem. Marge liked everyone. She believed in the goodness of people until they proved her wrong. It was one part of her new faith that Annie hadn't fully come to accept.

A short time later there was a knock at her door. What if it was him? If he had the nerve to invade her room, she would give him an earful. "Who is it?"

"It's Marge. Are you okay, Annie?"

"Come in."

Marge eased open the door. "I know you must be upset with me."

"I can't believe you invited him back. You know I don't want to see him."

"That's what you say, but that isn't the whole truth, is it?"

"I don't know what you mean."

"Honey, I've seen the way you look at him and I've also seen the way he looks at you."

"How is that?"

"Like he's found something rare and precious."

"You can't be serious." Did he look at her that way?

"It's the same way my husband looked at me when we first met."

"It's not me he's seeing. It's the baby."

Tilting her head to one side, Marge studied Annie's face. "No, I don't think he sees the baby when he looks at you. He sees the same woman I do. Someone who is incredibly strong but who doesn't yet believe in herself."

"I believe in God. That's enough."

"It's a wonderful start, but that isn't all it takes to live a Christian life."

"I'm trying, Marge."

"I know you are, sweetheart."

Looking down, Marge said, "This is going to sound very materialistic on my part, but I really do need this roof fixed before it falls in on us. He's willing to do it in exchange for a meal each evening he's here. And he's even going to get the shingles on base for me—at a discount that I couldn't turn down."

"So you're telling me that he is a caring and practical man and that I'm a fool to try and keep him out of my baby's life."

"I would never say that you were a fool. Annie, you're entitled to your feelings. I'm just asking you to take a closer look at them. Your past has made you distrustful of men, and with good reason, but you've turned your life around. You aren't the same woman who let men take advantage of you."

Annie managed a wry smile. "I'm not that woman any-more, but sometimes…I'm afraid she'll come back."

"She won't if you don't allow it. You have found God. He is your strength now. He will guide you in the right direction."

"Would that be toward or away from a certain corporal?"

Marge chuckled. "I don't know the answer to that, but I'm hoping the good Lord lets me get my roof fixed while you and he work it out."

The following evening Shane borrowed the unit's pick-up with the captain's permission and purchased the needed supplies at the Post Exchange. With the help of Lee and Avery, he soon had several large loads of new asphalt shingle bundles delivered and stacked at the back of Marge's house.

Crystal and Olivia watched the activity from the picnic table nearby. When the men finished unloading the last of the materials, Olivia jumped up. "Would you like something to drink?"

Shane wiped the sweat from his brow with the back of his sleeve. "That would be great."

"We have soda, iced tea or water. What would you like?"

"Iced tea for me," he answered.

Olivia took everyone's orders and hurried into the house. In a few minutes she returned with a large glass of tea and two sodas. Lee and Avery had already made themselves comfortable on either side of Crystal at the picnic table. After giving the men their drinks, Olivia brought Shane his glass.

Leaning against the lowered tailgate of the truck, he took a long swallow of the icy drink and sighed with pleasure, then glanced up at Annie's window. He had half hoped to catch her spying on him.

Olivia hopped onto the tailgate beside him. "Annie's in the living room, studying."

"Studying what?"

"Stuff about becoming a counselor like my mom."

"Annie's going to school?"

"She goes to classes on the weekend. She says she can't afford to go to school full-time. Her job doesn't pay well and her tips aren't always good."

"I think it's great that she wants to get an education." He wasn't sure if it was right to encourage Olivia to talk about Annie, but he was hungry for any information he could get about her.

"That's what Mom says. Why is Annie pretending that she doesn't like you?"

He looked at his little confidante in surprise. "What makes you say that?"

"Because she must have peeked out the kitchen window fifty times while you were working back here earlier. For someone who's says she doesn't want you around, she sure checks on you a lot."

"That's interesting." So Annie wasn't indifferent. That was good news. He took another sip of his tea. Maybe it was time he stopped pursuing her. Maybe it was time to see if she would make the next move. He finished his drink and handed the glass back.

Olivia took it and rolled the amber tumbler between her

palms. Slanting him a quizzical look, she asked, "Do you like Annie?"

"I do."

"Why don't you two go out on a date or something?"

"It's not as easy as it sounds."

"Why not?"

"It's…complicated."

She held up one hand. "Pleease! If one more person tells me that, I'm going to scream."

Over the next several days Annie spent her hours at work torn between her dread of going home because Shane would be there and an equally irrational eagerness to see him again. The first two evenings he had worked on the roof, she had stayed shut up in her room, claiming she needed to study—as if anyone could concentrate with the nail gun going off almost constantly.

Each night when darkness fell, he put up his tools and the ladder and left without making any attempt to see her. He even declined the meals Marge offered. Knowing he was doing the work he had promised without any compensation—because of her—began to gnaw at Annie's conscience.

On the third evening she sat at the table with Marge, Olivia and Crystal and listened to his footsteps overhead. The smell of broiled hamburgers, dill pickles and potato salad reminded Annie of the picnics her parents had taken her on when she was a kid. Suddenly she couldn't stand it any longer.

Loading a second plate with a generous helping of food,

she excused herself and carried it outside. Walking to the ladder, she looked up and called, "Shane, I brought you something to eat."

The silence lasted about five seconds.

"Thanks, but I'm fine."

"You've been working for hours. It won't kill you to take a break and eat a bite."

"The longer I work, the sooner I'll have this done." *Boom, boom, boom.*

Balancing the plate with care, she began to climb the ladder one-handed. She reached the top and was setting his plate on the sloping roof when his startled voice rang out. "What do you think you're doing?"

"I'm bringing you supper."

He grabbed the ladder with both hands to steady it. His face was only inches from hers. "Are you nuts? You shouldn't be climbing up here in your condition."

"I'm pregnant, not acrophobic."

"Not what?" His eyes were wide and he had a death grip on the ladder beams.

"Acrophobia is a fear of heights."

"Okay, let's just say I get that when I see a pregnant woman fifteen feet above the ground. Please get down."

"Will you eat?"

"I'm trying to get this finished before it rains again."

"There's no rain in the forecast for the next thirty minutes, so you have time for dinner. I'm not going down until you eat."

"I can't eat. My hands are busy holding this ladder so you don't fall."

"The ladder is perfectly sound. You've been going up

and down it for days." She tried to pry one of his hands loose but only managed to get his pointer finger undone. His strength surprised her.

"Okay, you win." The sudden change in the timbre of his voice sent waves of tingles racing across her nerve endings. He let go of the ladder and closed his grip over her hand.

"Good." Oh, that had sounded breathless even to her ears. The rough texture of his skin against hers only served to make her more aware of her femininity. The size of his hand made her feel small and protected, not frightened.

He sank back cross-legged onto the roof, letting her hand slip out of his in a slow caress. "I eat and you get down. Do we have a deal?"

Clearing her throat, she nodded. "We do."

Picking up the burger, he stuffed it in his mouth in two bites. Pointing downward, he mumbled, "Go."

"Are you trying to choke yourself?"

Chewing momentarily silenced him, but his eyes spoke volumes as he glared at her. Swallowing at last, he said, "Get your feet on the ground. That's an order!"

She opened her mouth to object to his manner, but he shot to his knees and gripped the ladder again. "I know how to do a fireman's carry. Don't make me prove it."

A dignified retreat seemed like her best choice. "I'm going."

Backing down the ladder with care, she stepped off the last rung and moved to the side. A moment later he slid down without using his feet and landed beside her.

Impressed, she asked, "Where did you learn to do that?"

"My foster father ran a roofing business. When I was old enough, I worked with him."

"What happened to your birth parents?"

"My mom died of cancer when I was eleven."

"I'm sorry."

He shrugged. "It was a long time ago."

She couldn't help but notice that he didn't mention his father.

"What about you?" he asked, walking toward the picnic table. Unbuckling his tool belt, he tossed it onto the wooden surface.

"My parents live on Long Island. We don't keep in touch."

"Why not? I'm sorry—that's none of my business."

It wasn't something she normally talked about. But then, her relationship with Shane could be called anything but normal. Without knowing exactly why, she wanted him to understand who she had been.

"My addiction made me a very destructive person. I hurt my parents in a lot of ways. I can't tell you how many times they got me out of jail or picked me up at some hospital. I took money from them every chance I got. When they stopped keeping cash in the house, I stole their credit cards. I ruined them. My mom lost her job. Eventually they even lost their house. In the end, they had to cut me out of their lives. I have a younger brother. I know they did it for his sake. I don't blame them now, but I did for a very long time."

"Do they know you're sober now?"

"I wrote them a letter last year to tell them how sorry I was and that I had found God, but they didn't write back.

I still hope someday that they will find it in their hearts to forgive me."

   "So what happened the day we met, Annie? What made you go into that bar?"

Chapter Eight

Annie crossed her arms over her chest as she faced Shane. Sharing her experiences with other recovering addicts was one thing. They understood. How much of what she had been through could Shane understand? Would telling him make him doubt her ability to be a good mother? No matter what he might think, she knew that this baby was God's way of helping her overcome her disease. For her child's sake, she would never drink again.

"Why did I get smashed the night we met? I wish I had a plausible explanation. I wish I had a good reason, but the fact is, I don't. I'm an alcoholic, Shane. I don't need an excuse to drink."

He settled his hip onto the table edge. "Something must have happened. You said that you had been sober for almost a year before then."

"The day we met I had just been fired from my job. It wasn't a great job, but I needed it. I really felt like I was making some progress turning my life around and then— pow!—I'm unemployed."

"Why were you fired?"

"The little company I was doing secretarial work for needed to make cutbacks. Last hired, first fired. It was as simple as that. Life wasn't being fair. God had failed me. I didn't know what to do. So I returned to the one thing I knew would make me feel better."

"Only it didn't help."

It was tempting to share her painful journey to sobriety with this man, but she held back. She wasn't ready to expose her innermost fears and doubts to him. Her failure was between herself and God.

"No, it didn't help. It made things worse. Just look at me now."

"I think you look fine. In fact, I think you look amazing."

His compliment caught her off guard. "Are you sure you're putting those shingles on right? Because I don't think you see so well."

"I see a young woman in a difficult situation who is making a positive change in her life. That is an amazing thing. My son or daughter could do a lot worse in the mother department."

He sounded so sincere. Her usual flippant comeback didn't materialize. Instead she murmured, "Thank you."

He straightened and reached for his tool belt. "I'd better get back to work. The roof won't replace itself."

"But you didn't finish your dinner." Her desire to stay and talk with him surprised her as much as his compliment had. For some reason, being near him didn't make her as uncomfortable as she had expected. Instead his nearness left her feeling happy and a little giddy, if she were being honest.

Shane rubbed one hand over his jaw. "Truthfully, I ate before I came over tonight. But thanks for the hamburger. It was good."

"Did you even taste it?"

"I was too afraid you'd fall."

He cared about her and about the baby. The knowledge wrapped itself like a warm blanket around her heart.

"Tomorrow evening you'll join us at the table, and that is an order, Corporal. I know you agreed to do this work in exchange for some home-cooked meals. If you don't start eating them, Marge is going to feel compelled to pay you."

He sketched a quick salute. "Yes, ma'am. I'll be here tomorrow and I promise to bring my appetite."

"Good. You'll be expected to clean your plate."

"I will."

Picking up his tool belt, he slung it around his waist but paused in the act of buckling it to look at her. "Unless you're having okra or goat. I can't promise to eat those."

"You're kidding, right?"

"I'm deadly serious. I never joke about okra."

"Who eats goat?"

"Lots of people," he said with a straight face.

"Eew!"

"My thoughts exactly. I guess it's safe to assume those two things won't be on the menu tomorrow?"

"You're pretty safe with that assumption, but just in case, I'll let Marge know that you don't eat goat."

"Or okra."

She nodded slowly. "Or okra. I'll go cross it off the shopping list right now."

"Thanks." He finished buckling on his tools and headed for the ladder.

The following day Shane arrived at Marge's house in high spirits. His conversation with Annie had given him a new measure of hope. She wasn't averse to spending time with him. He would even go so far as to say that she had enjoyed their talk. He certainly had enjoyed his time with her—once she was safely off the ladder.

Now, if he could only sway her to his way of thinking. A child needed a mother *and* a father. There had to be some way for them to work out their differences.

Opening the trunk of his car, he pulled out a roll of nails for the nail gun he had rented for the project. Any work was easier if a man had the right tools for the job. If only he could figure out what tools he needed to convince Annie he was father material. Spending time with her was the key. This roofing project would only take a few more evenings. Somehow he had to get her to agree to see him after it was done. So far, he knew that independence, education, helping others and her faith were things Annie valued deeply. He valued the same things—all but faith. Why was it so important to her?

Annie drove up just as he closed his trunk lid. Parking behind him, she turned off the engine, but it chugged several times before it finally died. Crystal jumped out of the passenger side and hurried into the house with only the briefest of waves in his direction. He walked toward Annie.

"You should get this vehicle looked at," he suggested when she stepped out of the car.

"I will. It just has to keep running until payday." Closing her eyes, she put her hands on her hips. A grimace crossed her face as she leaned backward.

"You're home late. Tough day?" he asked, walking to stand beside her.

"I've had worse."

"Turn around."

"What for?"

"Just do it."

After giving him a long, suspicious stare, she finally did as he'd asked. Placing his hands on her shoulders, he began to massage her tense muscles.

She stiffened for a second, but then she gradually relaxed. After a few more moments her head lolled forward. "Mmm, I'll give you until next Tuesday to stop that. Do you do feet?"

"If you need horseshoes, I'm your man."

She giggled. "The last thing I need is iron shoes. My feet hurt enough as it is."

Shane couldn't believe how much it pleased him to hear her laugh. After a minute she stepped away from his massage, and he let his empty hands fall to his sides. The urge to pull her into his arms and hold her close was almost painful in its intensity. It took all his willpower not to act on the impulse. This wasn't the time or the place. Instinctively he knew he would lose what little trust he had gained. "Okay, no new shoes from my forge."

The rush of color in her cheeks told him she wasn't indifferent to his touch.

"How's the roof coming?" she asked quickly.

"I should be able to finish next week. The gables and the steep pitch make for slow going." That and the fact that he wasn't in any hurry to complete the project.

"You are staying for supper tonight, aren't you?"

"I'm looking forward to it."

"If I get a move on, it will be ready in about an hour."

"You aren't cooking tonight after working so late, are you? You look exhausted."

"Food won't fix itself because the cook is tired. We take turns with the chores and tonight is my night to make supper. I'll manage."

He clearly remembered Olivia and Crystal laughing at the idea of Annie cooking. "Maybe we should call out for pizza or something."

She scowled at him. "Are you afraid I can't cook a decent meal because I'm a little tired?"

He found himself on the defensive and tried to back-pedal. "That's not what I was saying. I just thought that you should be taking it easy. You are pregnant, after all."

She smacked her palm against her forehead. "Wow, I completely forgot that. Thank you for reminding me. How did I get this way? Oh, that's right—you helped." Stepping toward him, she poked her finger into his chest. "For your information, being pregnant doesn't affect the way I cook, either."

He held up both hands. "Whoa, I'm not sure how I got here. Can we go back to the point where I didn't have my foot in my mouth and you were happy to see me?"

Glaring, she crossed her arms over her chest. "Was I ever happy to see you?"

"I thought so—but I've been wrong before."

She arched one eyebrow. "I'm sure you have."

"Yes, a lot. Well, maybe not a lot but often. Sometimes."

He gestured toward the house. "Okay, I'm going to climb up on the roof with my hammer now and try to pry my foot loose."

"You do that."

"I'll just go do that," he muttered as he picked up the roll of nails and headed for the backyard.

A little over an hour later Annie placed her tuna casserole in front of Shane and took her place opposite him at the table.

"It sure smells good," he said for the third time since he'd come in.

How a man his size managed to look like a repentant first-grader was beyond her understanding. She took pity on him and gave him a small smile. "I hope you enjoy it."

Nodding, he grinned in return. "I'm sure I will."

From the head of the table Marge asked, "Where is Crystal?"

Annie glanced at the clock. "She said she had a few errands to run and not to wait for her."

A small crease appeared between Marge's brows. "She's been gone a lot lately. Did she borrow your car again?"

"Yes, but I don't mind. She puts gas in it. Don't worry—she knows she has to be back before the meeting tonight."

The smile Marge tried for looked forced. "Still, I think I should talk to her. I have the feeling that something isn't right."

Smiling at her, Annie said, "You worry too much."

"Maybe you're right." Marge looked at Shane. "Would you like to lead us in prayer tonight?"

"Me?" His voice didn't quite squeak, but his apprehension was painfully clear.

Olivia giggled but quickly subdued her mirth at her mother's quelling stare.

Looking sheepish, he said, "I'm afraid I don't know many blessings for eating except the one that goes 'Good food, good meat'…and I don't think that's what you had in mind."

It was Annie's turn to choke back a laugh. Marge scowled at her, then turned her attention to Shane. "There aren't any rules. Just tell God what you have to be thankful for."

"Okay." Taking a deep breath, he bowed his head and closed his eyes. "God, Thank You for the food on this table."

Annie felt his gaze. When she opened her eyes, she found him staring at her.

"Thanks, too, for giving me the chance to know these special people," he said quietly.

Hoping their interplay and her blush would go unnoticed, Annie glanced toward Marge. Mercifully Marge's perceptive eyes were still closed and her head was bowed in prayer.

"And thanks for not letting me fall off the roof today. Amen," he added in a rush.

"Amen," Marge echoed, but not before Annie saw the tiniest twitch at the corner of her mouth.

"We still can't thank you enough for fixing our roof," Marge said as everyone began filling their plates.

"It's my pleasure. It's been kind of fun doing something besides taking care of horses and riding."

"I'd never get tired of taking care of a horse if I had one," Olivia asserted, passing a bowl of peas and pearl onions to her mother.

"Don't be too sure of that," Shane said. "They take a lot more looking after than you might imagine. Especially horses that work as hard as ours do."

"Annie tells me that you'll be leaving soon." Marge spooned a portion of vegetables onto her plate and handed the bowl to Annie.

"My tour with the Commanding General's Mounted Color Guard will be finished the end of July. After that I'll be returning to my regular unit."

"Will you, like, be driving tanks and things?" Olivia asked.

"Mostly I'll be fixing helicopters. It's what I do."

"That's cool." Olivia forked a bit of casserole into her mouth.

"Shane is being transferred to a base in Germany," Annie added. That, among other things, was part of the reason she resisted his requests to be involved with the baby. He wouldn't even be in the country, so how could she include him? She couldn't—even if she wanted to—which she didn't.

Olivia turned her attention to Annie. "Are you going to find out if you're having a boy or a girl tomorrow?"

Glancing toward Shane, Annie caught the sudden interest in his eyes. Looking down at her plate, she separated a small piece of carrot from the noodles with her fork. "I see my doctor tomorrow, but the sonogram isn't until next week. I haven't decided if I want to know or not."

"Why not?" Shane asked.

"I'm not sure. It seems a little like peeking at my Christmas presents three months early. I think I'd rather wait until the big day."

"What about you, Shane?" Olivia asked. "Do you want a girl or a boy?"

"I'd like to know that everything is okay. Whether it's a boy or a girl really doesn't matter."

"I hope it's a girl," Olivia said. "But a boy would be nice, too."

Annie looked up to see Shane hiding a smile. He winked and said, "I'm sure it will be one or the other."

Olivia rolled her eyes at him. "Well, duh! Have you picked out names yet, Annie?"

Watching Shane's face, Annie said, "I've always liked the name Joshua for a boy. I haven't decided on a girl's name yet."

Shane met her gaze. "Joshua. Josh. It's a good name."

"What about you, Shane?" Marge asked. "Have you given any thought to names for the baby?"

Shaking his head, he looked down. "I haven't. I think that should be Annie's decision, but I do have one request. If it's a girl, please don't name her Pat or Jane."

Perplexed, Annie asked, "And why not?"

"Something tells me that any daughter of yours will already have a predisposition to stubbornness without being named after the mules in the Commanding General's

Mounted Color Guard." The humor in his voice made Annie grin in return.

"Very well, I'll take Pat and Jane off my list of girl's names."

"Thanks, that's all I ask."

Annie's smile faded. If only that were true. But it wasn't. He was asking for so much more—more than she could give. Yet every day she found herself questioning that conviction.

What would sharing the burdens and the joys of raising a child with Shane be like? More and more she found herself imagining them all together. It was foolish, but deep in the corners of her heart she wished it could be real.

When the meal was finished, Marge pushed back her chair. "I'm sorry to eat and run, but I'm manning the phones at the crisis center tonight. Olivia, I expect you to mind Annie at the meeting tonight."

"Aw, Mom, do I still have to go? You know I'm not going to pull a stunt like that again."

"I never expected you to pull a 'stunt' like that in the first place. So, yes, you still have to go. I want you to see exactly what kind of harm alcohol can do to people's lives."

"I already know!"

"I don't think you do. You're going with Annie tonight and that's final. Maybe after this you'll think twice about following someone else's lead when you know it's wrong."

"I already said I was sorry. It's been a week. I can't understand why I'm still grounded from seeing my friends or why I have to go to some gross AA meeting with people I don't even know."

"That's enough, Olivia."

Looking as if she wanted to protest further, Olivia opened her mouth, but Marge forestalled her. "Not another word."

"Fine. I'll be in my room. Call me when you're ready to go, Annie."

Olivia stomped out of the kitchen without a backward glance. Rising, Annie picked up her plate and stacked it on top of Marge's. The clacking of stoneware on stoneware sounded unusually loud in the sudden tense silence.

Marge sent both Shane and Annie apologetic looks. "I'm sorry about that. Annie, I should be the one taking her. I shouldn't pawn off the task on you."

"You aren't pawning anything off on me. I'm glad to do it. Besides, it might feel less like punishment to her if you aren't there."

"That's what I'm hoping. If I went with you, she'd only spend her time sighing and glaring at me. I don't know why she's so angry. I'm the one who should be mad."

Annie set the dishes down to give her friend a quick hug. "From personal experience I can tell you Olivia's anger is more about being disappointed in her own behavior than about being mad at you. She'll get over it."

"I hope so. Shane, I'm sorry that you had to witness my daughter's surly behavior."

"That's okay, Mrs. Lilly. I wish my dad had cared enough to ground me when I was Olivia's age. If you ladies will excuse me, I'm going to get back to work while I have some daylight left."

Annie nodded and watched him leave by the back door. As she began to gather up the rest of the plates, Marge stopped her with a hand on her arm. "He seems like a good man, Annie. Are you sure you're doing the right thing by excluding him from your baby's life?"

Annie glanced toward the door to make sure he was gone. "It's the right thing. He'll forget all about us in a few months."

"I don't think so."

"I'd like to believe that, but I just can't. I need to do this myself. I have to be strong for this child. I can't risk depending on someone who'll let me down when I need him."

"I know you've been in bad relationships before."

"Yes, I have, and every time I thought they were men I could depend on, but they weren't. When things got rocky, they all took off, and I spiraled deeper into depression and drinking because of it. I got sober with God's help. I'll stay sober with God's help and because this baby needs me."

"I'm sure you will, Annie. You've come so far already. But don't count out the support of your friends."

"I don't. I know that you and Crystal and the people at group will always be here for me. That's enough."

Marge glanced at the clock. "I wish we had more time to talk about this, but I have to get going."

"Marge, I'm fine. Stop worrying. I don't want to make you late."

"Are you sure that you're all right with taking Olivia?"

"Of course I am. Now, get going. There's no telling when God will send some other needy soul in your direction."

Smiling, Marge nodded and headed for the living room. At the doorway she paused and looked back. "I'm really glad He sent you to me. You're a special person, Annie."

"You're nowhere near as glad as I am."

"I wish you would consider the fact that God may have sent Shane into your life for a reason."

"I don't need him."

"That may be true, but what if *he* needs *you?*"

Chapter Nine

It was beginning to get dark by the time Shane finished the section of the roof he had been working on. After climbing down, he removed the ladder and carried it to the garden shed at the back of the yard. He then brought his tools around to his car parked at the side of the house. Since Marge's coupe was gone, he assumed that she had already left for the evening. Annie's car was gone, too.

He couldn't help but wonder if Olivia was giving Annie the same attitude about attending the AA meeting that she had given her mother earlier. He hoped not. Annie deserved praise for her efforts, not criticism.

After opening his trunk, he threw his gear in and closed the lid. He heard the sound of Marge's front door opening and glanced toward the house. To his surprise, he saw Annie standing in the open doorway.

"I'm done for the night," he called, and gave her a brief wave.

Advancing down the steps, she paused on the walk. "I thought I heard a car door. I was hoping it was Crystal. She promised to be home before we had to leave for the meeting."

He took a step closer. "She isn't back yet?"

"No." She crossed her arms over her chest and stared down the street.

He walked toward her. "Maybe she had car trouble. Do you want me to wait?"

"Thanks, but I'm sure she'll be here any minute. She knows that I'm leading the group discussion tonight and that Olivia is coming with us. I've tried her cell phone, but she has it turned off. If she had car trouble, I'm sure she would have called."

"Maybe she just forgot the time."

"Maybe."

"Why don't I give you and Olivia a lift?"

"It's out of your way, but thank you."

He narrowed the distance between them until he was close enough to see the worry in her eyes. "Junction City isn't a big town, so I'm sure your meeting isn't *that* far out of my way."

She glanced back toward the door of the house. "I hate to impose."

The evening breeze carried the scent of her perfume to him. The sweet fragrance stirred a recollection from his early childhood. He leaned closer. She didn't pull away. Closing his eyes, he inhaled deeply and tried to capture the elusive memory.

"White flowers." He didn't realize he had spoken aloud until he heard her soft indrawn breath.

He opened his eyes and met her uncertain gaze. Large and luminous in the growing dusk, her eyes were filled with bewilderment and another emotion that sent his pulse racing.

"You smell like the white flowers my mother grew in hanging baskets on our front porch. I don't remember what they were called."

"Jasmine," she whispered softly.

He reached out and stroked her cheek with his fingertips. "Jasmine—that's right. I remember breathing in their fragrance and trying to so hard not to breathe out."

With sudden clarity Shane knew that this moment would become a treasured memory for him. He longed to capture and keep everything exactly as it was now. The way her long braid hung over her shoulder, begging him to run his hand down its soft length. The way the wind teased a few strands of her hair loose to flutter beside her small, delicate ears. The way her lips curved with the hint of a smile.

Oh, yes, the smells of a summer evening and jasmine would forever remind him of her.

If she only knew how much he wanted to stay near her, to help her, to make her smile. The astonishing thing was that none of the feelings running through him had anything to do with the fact that she was carrying his baby.

Annie struggled to calm her pounding heart. The touch of his hand on her cheek crystallized her jumbled feelings. In spite of her best efforts to remain indifferent, she was falling in love with this man. Head over heels in love. She longed to follow the flow of her emotions and step into his arms, but some small part of her brain recognized doing that was a recipe for disaster.

The streetlight on the corner flickered on. He let his hand fall to his side. "It's a good memory."

She stood there, looking up at him with a strange sort of wonder. Finally she said, "Good memories are something to cherish."

He drew a deep breath and smiled as he shoved his hands in his pockets. "So can I give you and Olivia a ride?"

His nonchalance helped steady her shaky nerves and forced her to think about the matter at hand. She didn't want to accept his offer. She needed time away from him. Thinking was hard to do when he stood so close. She glanced at her watch and then down the still-empty street.

It didn't seem that she had a choice, not if she was going to keep her commitment to her AA group and to Marge. Hoping she sounded as unaffected as he did, she said, "If you're sure you don't mind?"

"I don't mind at all."

"Let me leave a note for Crystal, then Olivia and I will be right out."

She turned away and hurried up the steps, but at the doorway she paused and looked back. "You don't have to do this. You don't owe me anything."

"Annie, you might feel that way, but I don't."

"How can I make you see that isn't true?"

"You can't. Go get Olivia and come on, or you will be late. Didn't you say you were the speaker?"

"If I weren't, I wouldn't be accepting your offer."

"How'd you get to be so stubborn?"

"Practice. How did you get that way?"

"It comes naturally—just like my charm."

Grinning, she turned away and entered the house. Olivia

was waiting on the sofa. Pulling a piece of paper and a pen from the small pine desk by the window, Annie said, "Crystal isn't back yet."

Olivia sat up hopefully. "Does that mean we aren't going?"

"No, Shane has offered to drive us."

Sinking back into the cushions, she mumbled, "Great."

"It won't be bad, I promise." Annie finished her note and posted it on the message board the family used in the hallway.

When she came back into the living room, Olivia rose from the couch and headed to the door. "I guess if there's no way out of it, I might as well get it over with."

"That's the spirit." Annie patted her shoulder as she walked past.

Shane waited beside the car. He opened the door, pulled the seat forward and waved them in. "Ladies, your chariot awaits."

"I'll ride in back," Olivia said before squeezing herself into the sports car's rear seat. Annie was happy to let her. Getting into and out of tight places was harder now that her jeans were getting snug. Soon she'd need to invest in some maternity clothes.

After Shane shut the door, Annie laid a hand on her slightly rounded tummy. The idea of outgrowing her limited wardrobe had once made her frown, but tonight the thought brought only a glow of happiness. This baby was changing everything.

Shane opened his door and slid behind the wheel. He glanced toward her, his eyes settling on her hand. "Are we ready?"

"I'm getting there," she answered, and smiled at him.

"That's a good thing," he said softly, meeting her gaze with a smile of his own. Knowing that he understood boosted her happiness a notch higher.

From the backseat Olivia muttered, "I'm as ready as I'll ever be."

Exchanging amused looks with Shane, Annie turned and pulled her seat belt out and fastened it with a click.

Following Annie's directions, it took Shane less than ten minutes to reach their destination. As he pulled into the parking lot of a small, modern brick church, he noted with surprise that there were several dozen cars already parked close to the building.

Annie opened her door. "Thank you for bringing us, Shane."

"I don't see your car in this bunch. It looks like Crystal hasn't made it yet. Why don't I stick around in case you need a ride home?"

"That won't be necessary."

Olivia spoke up for the first time since they'd left the house. "I'd feel better if he stayed."

Shane smiled at her. "Okay, maybe I'll stick around and see what AA is all about."

"That would be awesome. Thank you."

He could see that Annie was torn, but in the end she nodded. "This is an open meeting. Not all AA groups operate that way, but we do. You're welcome to stay."

Inside the building, Annie led the way to a small meeting room. Gray metal folding chairs were set in rows facing a table with a small podium in the center. About half the chairs were already filled. A second table along the wall held a few plates of cookies, a coffee urn and several stacks of foam cups.

Shane scanned the faces of the people already assembled in the room. There were two young women chatting in the front row. One, a blonde in her early thirties wearing white sandals, crisp khaki pants and a pale blue sweater, looked as if she had just dropped her kids off at soccer practice. The woman beside her wore a short black skirt and a black tank top and sported maroon streaks in her black hair. Behind them sat a man in a business suit who looked to be in his fifties. Three rows back, a woman with gray hair and a brightly flowered red dress looked as if she should be baking cookies for her grandchildren.

"You can sit anywhere," Annie said, gesturing toward the chairs.

Olivia grabbed Shane's arm. "Let's sit in the back."

"I think we should sit up front and offer Annie a little moral support, don't you?"

"I don't want to sit up there where people will be looking at me and wondering if I'm the youngest alcoholic on record. Please—let's sit in back."

Annie nodded to the two of them. "Thank you for your offer of support, Shane, but let Olivia sit wherever she is comfortable."

"That would be at home on the sofa," the teen muttered. She sent an uneasy glance around the room and took a step closer to Annie.

Placing a finger under Olivia's jaw, Annie turned the girl's face back to her own. "Our actions have consequences. Your mother wants you to see that."

"I do. Honest."

"I know you believe that, but I think you'll see it much more clearly after tonight."

"Annie!" An elderly man wearing a short-sleeved black shirt and black slacks waved from across the room. Leaving the refreshment table, he came toward them.

Casting Annie a pleading look, Olivia begged in a whisper, "Don't tell Pastor Hill why I'm here."

"Of course I won't. That's entirely up to you."

Engulfing Annie in a bear hug, the man beamed. "My dear, it's good to see you." He reared back. "And I see you've brought Olivia with you. Welcome, child. Have you come to see firsthand the good work that God has led us to do?"

"Sort of, Pastor Hill."

"Excellent. And who is this?" He extended his hand toward Shane.

Taking the beefy hand, Shane noted the strength in the man's grip, as well as the friendliness in his eyes. "I'm Shane Ross, sir, a friend of Annie's."

"Any friend of Annie's is a friend of mine. She is a true pearl, isn't she?"

"I have to agree."

Sneaking a peek at the object of their conversation, he noted a blush adding color to her cheeks. Taking pity on her, he said, "If you'll excuse us, sir, we were just about to find a seat."

"Of course. Oh, there's Manny. I'm so glad he's here. This is his tenth straight meeting. I must go and see how he's doing."

Shane took Olivia's hand and tugged her toward the

back of the room. "Come on, kiddo, let's sit down before all the good seats are taken."

Choosing the last chair on the center aisle, he settled himself on the hard metal seat, while Olivia slumped in the chair next to him.

A few moments later Pastor Hill stepped up to the podium and rapped on it with his knuckles. The hubbub of voices died away. "It's time we got started. I'd like to welcome all of you here tonight. My name is Gerry and I'm an alcoholic."

A chorus of voices called out, "Hello, Gerry."

Olivia straightened in her chair. She exchanged a startled look with Shane, then turned her attention to the front of the room.

Pastor Hill nodded and leaned forward, bracing his hands on the wooden stand. "Thank you. Tonight I'm going to turn the meeting over to Annie, who will lead our discussion. If you have questions, please raise your hand. Annie?"

"Thank you, Pastor Hill."

She waited until he took a seat in the front row, then she looked out over the crowd. "My name is Annie and I'm an alcoholic."

After the tide of greetings died away, she continued. "I see several new faces here and it gladdens my heart. While you may be here because of a court order or because a family member forced you to come, I want to tell you all that you have made an important first step. What you are going through, I have been through. I know that, as a newcomer, I was ashamed to be seen at an AA meeting despite knowing that nearly everyone present was also an alcoholic.

"Why? Because I didn't think I needed help. I knew that my drinking had messed up my life, but I hadn't yet admitted that I couldn't control it. Admitting that we are helpless against alcohol is painful, but it is the only way we can gain control over the disease that is destroying us and those we love."

As she spoke about her addiction and the suffering she had endured because of it, Shane found his respect for her growing by leaps and bounds. While he freely admitted that he found her attractive on a physical level, he faced the fact that he hadn't begun to see the true depth and inner beauty of this remarkable woman.

At her direction, members of the assembly stood and introduced themselves and began to talk about their personal journeys. The grandmother's name was Barbara and she had been drinking since she was twenty. She talked about how her husband left her and took their children and how she hadn't spoken to any of them in over ten years.

The woman with maroon streaks said her name was Nadia. She started drinking at the age of eleven. The day she turned twenty-six, she plowed her car into an empty school bus. The thought that it could have been full of children finally made her seek help.

The man in the suit hadn't been so fortunate. His name was Bill and his wife and daughter died in an accident that happened when he was driving drunk. Even then, he admitted, it took him another fifteen years to hit bottom and seek help.

Not everyone spoke. A few people passed without sharing. Two young men came in late. One of them waited only five minutes before hurrying out the door again.

As Shane listened to the stories and struggles of those around him, one clear thing took shape: all of these people had turned to God when everything else in life had failed them. Like Annie, they gave God credit for their healing and their strength. This was God presented not as some being above the clouds but as a vital presence. In his heart he knew he had been missing out on something important and he decided he wanted to know more.

When the time was up, Pastor Hill stood and faced the group. "Before we close, I'd like us to bow our heads and ask the Lord guidance for all of us here this evening."

Shane bowed his head with the others as Pastor Hill began to pray. "God, I offer my heart and my soul to You. I am but clay, waiting for the master's hand to mold me into a vessel of Your purpose. Help me to do Your will. Only through You can I achieve victory over my addiction. Let me bear witness to Your loving power. If I stumble, do not forsake me. Guide me to help others in need the way I have been helped. May I do Your will always. Amen."

Deeply moved by the words, Shane knew that he had to learn more about the faith shared by these people.

Annie helped herself to a glass of punch at the refreshment table and chided herself for being a coward. Shane had spent a long time talking to Pastor Hill at the back of the room, but he and Olivia were back in their seats with cups in one hand and cookies in the other. By visiting with several of her friends, Annie had managed to avoid making eye contact with him until now.

What had he thought of her story? Was he disappointed that she had wasted the education her parents had worked so hard to provide and drunk her way through college instead? Had he been repulsed by the knowledge that she had lived with several different men? Would he think she was an unfit mother now that he knew she had taken an overdose of painkillers and tried to end her life before she found God?

She drew a deep breath. *Wallowing in guilt and self-blame doesn't help. I have learned to live in the solution and not dwell in the problem.*

Gathering her courage, she crossed the room and sat down by Olivia. "Well, what did you think?"

Olivia looked up, her eyes as wide a saucers. "Did you hear that woman say she started drinking when she was eleven? I couldn't believe it."

"That's part of the reason your mother wanted you to come tonight. She wanted you to understand how dangerous a drug alcohol can be."

"I almost cried when Bill talked about drinking to make it through his daughter's funeral." Olivia looked around and lowered her voice. "And Pastor Hill—why would a minister need to drink?"

"Pastors are human, too. They have the same problems and burdens as—perhaps even more than—the rest of us. Alcohol seems to make those problems go away, but in reality it doesn't help. It only hurts. Part of our dependence is psychological, but a large part of it is physical. Our bodies process it differently. We truly can't stop after one drink."

"But you stopped," Shane chimed in at last.

"Yes, I did."

Tilting his head to the side, he studied her for a long moment, then asked, "Is there a risk that your son or daughter will have the same disease?"

Chapter Ten

Annie tried to read Shane's face. "Are you asking if our baby will inherit my alcoholism?"

"That's a possibility, isn't it?"

"It is, but it's not the only possibility. Not every child of an alcoholic becomes an alcoholic."

"How do you plan to deal with that risk?"

At his question, her heart sank. He wasn't asking how they could face such difficulty together, he'd asked how *she* planned to deal with it. In one sentence the child had become *hers* again. The pain of his withdrawal cut surprisingly deep, although she had known all along that something like this would happen. She wasn't perfect, so her baby might not be perfect.

If only he hadn't made her dream of more. Without even realizing it, she had begun to lean on him. Now she stumbled to regain her emotional balance. Biting her bottom lip until she could speak without crying, she laced her fingers together over the roundness of her belly.

"Annie, are you okay?" Olivia asked.

Swallowing hard, Annie nodded. "I'm fine." She would be. With God's help, she would be.

She raised her eyes and met Shane's without flinching. "I'll face that risk by being honest. By raising my child inside a firm foundation of faith. And by making sure that the lines of communication always stay open."

He nodded, but she had to wonder if he even understood. He wasn't a man of faith

Olivia spoke up again. "If you don't mind, I'm going to grab a couple of cookies before we head home."

Annie smiled at her. "Grab one for me, too."

The door to the meeting room opened. Annie looked over and saw Crystal step inside. One look at her friend's apprehensive face told Annie that something was wrong. She shot out of her chair and hurried to her. "Crystal, we were so worried about you. Is everything okay?"

Shoving her hands in the pockets of her cutoff jeans, Crystal avoided making eye contact. "I'm fine."

Concern for the younger woman prompted Annie to place a comforting arm around her shoulders. "What is it? What's wrong?"

"You're going to be so mad at me."

Puzzled, Annie tipped her head to the side. "Why would I be mad at you? Because you missed the meeting?"

"No."

"What then?"

"I kind of…loaned your car to Willie."

"You did what?" She stared at Crystal in astonishment.

"Willie needed a car to get to this job interview to-morrow," she said in a rush.

"You loaned my car to someone without asking me? Crystal, what were you thinking?"

"It's our day off. We don't have to go to work, so I didn't see the harm in letting him take the car for a day. You aren't mad at me, are you?"

"Yes, I am. You should have checked with me first. I have a doctor's appointment tomorrow. You knew that."

"Oh, man, I forgot about your appointment. I'm sorry, Annie. You and Marge are always talking about helping others in need. Willie needed my help. At the time it seemed like the right thing to do."

Sighing in defeat, Annie said, "I know you meant well, but you're going to have to call Willie and tell him you're sorry but I need my car tomorrow."

"That's kind of the thing—I can't. His job interview is out of town. He left right after he dropped me off here."

"Left for where?" Annie couldn't believe what she was hearing.

Crystal cringed as she said, "Kansas City."

"Kansas City!" The thought that she might never see her car again made Annie's knees weak. The old Ford wasn't much, but it was her most valuable possession.

Please, Lord, don't load anything else on my shoulders. I can't take it. She sank onto the closest chair.

Shane came across the room to stand beside her. "Is everything all right?"

She pressed a hand to her forehead. "No, it's not. But I can handle it."

Crystal brightened. "Hey, maybe Shane could take you to the doctor tomorrow."

"Did your poor excuse for a car give up the ghost?" he asked with a grin.

Scowling at Crystal, Annie spoke sharply. "Not exactly, but it seems that it is temporarily unavailable. Shane has his duties on base, Crystal. It was nice of him to bring us here tonight because you didn't get home on time and didn't bother to call, but I'm not asking him to do more."

"Yeah, I'm sorry about that. The time just sort of got away from me. Maybe Marge can take you—or one of the gals from work. Gina might do it. She's off tomorrow, too."

"Do you know Gina's phone number?"

"Well, no."

"Neither do I. And Marge has to work." Annie tried to calculate the cost of taking a cab out to the free clinic but realized she didn't have a clue how much it would cost.

Crystal asked, "Can't you reschedule?"

"It takes weeks to get an appointment." She hated to do it, but what choice did she have?

"I guess that leaves me," Shane interjected, sounding excessively happy.

"I'll manage something. Can we go home now?"

Looking disappointed, he nodded. "Sure."

She rose to say goodbye to Pastor Hill. A few minutes later she joined Shane outside. He stood waiting to open the car door for her. Crystal and Olivia were already in the backseat.

Stopping beside him, Annie tried to ignore the way her nerve endings came to life when he was near.

"Annie, I'm coming over to finish the roof tomorrow

anyway. I might as well give you a ride to your appointment." The husky tone of his voice sent her pulse racing.

Frowning, Annie couldn't help wondering why he was being so insistent. Had she jumped to the wrong conclusion earlier? Giving him the benefit of the doubt was hard. "Why are you going out of your way to help me?"

His eyebrows shot up. "Prenatal care is important. For your health, as well as for our baby. Why wouldn't I want to help?" Folding his arms over his chest, he said, "I don't get it. You accept help and support from people like Pastor Hill and from Marge, yet you act like my help is a bomb that will blow up in your face. Why is that?"

"Because that's the way my relationships with men have all ended in the past. They disintegrated when I needed them the most."

He leaned toward her so abruptly that Annie took a step back, but all he did was pull open the door. "I'm not one of those men, Annie. I'm not going anywhere."

Gazing into his eyes, she finally understood that what he said was true. He wasn't going to abandon her. She had been unfair to him from the start. She slid into the front seat of the car as the defensive wall she had built around her emotions crumbled, leaving her feeling weak and uncertain. He closed the door before she could think of what to say to him.

On the drive back to Marge's house Shane worked to rein in his anger. Teaching one of the unit's horses to fly would be easier than getting Annie to trust him. He had tried taking small steps to build a rapport with her, but each time he thought he was making progress, she retreated back into her shell like a startled turtle.

In spite of his words to the contrary, he had to wonder if he possessed the fortitude to stick with it. She didn't want him involved with their baby. Having parents at odds with each other had to be hard on a child. Would he only make life harder for his son or daughter by insisting Annie include him?

Crystal and Olivia were unusually quiet. Annie sat beside him staring straight ahead. He would have given a month's pay to know what she was thinking. Pulling up at a red light, he took the opportunity to glance over at her. She met his eyes and gave him a shy smile. Softly she said, "You're right and I'm sorry."

His annoyance dissipated, to be quickly replaced by remorse. "No, I'm the one who should be sorry. I need to stop forcing you into situations that make you uncomfortable."

"True, but you do have a way of getting a girl's attention."

"Is that good or bad?"

"Good, I think."

From the backseat Crystal said, "If the light gets any greener, you'll have to mow it."

Sending Annie a sheepish look, he shifted into gear and stepped on the gas. It took only a few more minutes to reach the house. As Olivia and Crystal went in, Annie hung back. When the others were out of earshot, she said, "Can I talk to you for a few minutes?"

Suddenly nervous, he shoved his hands in the front pockets of his jeans. "Sure."

"Shane, if you truly want to be involved with this baby, I'm not going to object any longer."

"Really? Thank you, Annie."

Nodding, she folded her arms across her middle. "I understand that you'll be overseas when I'm due to deliver, but I'll make sure that your name goes on the birth certificate."

"I'll put in for leave. There's a chance that they may let me come back then."

"That would be nice. I guess we can work out more of the details after he or she arrives."

"Details?"

"Visitation, holidays, summers when he's old enough. Details like that."

"Right." Hearing it put into words made it all sound so cold. Yet it was exactly what he had been fighting for. Now that he had it, where was the satisfaction?

"You don't sound happy."

"Of course I'm happy. I'm grateful, too. We'll make it work, I promise. This baby is going to know that he has two parents who love him."

"Or her."

"Or her," he agreed with a smile.

"So I'll see you tomorrow?"

"Bright and early. I want to get the roof done before I have to leave for our ride in Maddox the day after tomorrow."

"How long will you be gone?"

"Four days this time, but we've got a lot of appearances booked for the summer. It's our heavy travel season."

"Don't show up too early tomorrow. It's my day off and I intend to sleep in."

"How does ten sound?"

"About right."

"What time is your appointment?"

"Two o'clock at the free clinic over on Maple."

"I'll get you there. If what's-his-face doesn't get your car back to you tomorrow night, I'll leave you mine."

"No, I can't—"

He silenced her by placing a finger on her lips. "I'm not good at taking no for an answer. You need to get back and forth to work, and I'll be on horseback for three days. You might as well use my car."

She pulled his finger aside. "I started to say that I can't drive a stick shift."

"Oh. Well, we aren't taking the mules and the wagon with us. Maybe I could talk the captain into letting you use them."

"Ha-ha! Your offer is deeply appreciated, but I'm sure I'll have my car back."

"And if you don't, I'm leaving mine with you. You need transportation. I'll teach you how to drive a stick."

"I think I'd rather send Olivia to collect the mules."

"That works, too."

"Thanks for everything, Shane. I mean that."

"It was my pleasure, and I mean that. The meeting tonight opened my eyes to a lot of things. I admire you— and all the people there—for your bravery and your faith. The courage you displayed talking about your addiction showed uncommon valor."

He cupped her cheek with his hand. "You are something special, Annie Delmar, and I mean that, too."

Leaning in slowly, he waited for her to draw away or turn aside. When she didn't, he gently kissed her.

Chapter Eleven

"I saw you kiss him last night."

Startled, Annie looked up from her book to see Olivia leaning against the doorjamb of her bedroom. Dressed in blue cutoff jean shorts and a red sleeveless shirt, she managed to look both smugly teen and childlike at the same time. Raising one finger, she pointed to the ceiling. The sporadic *rat-tat-tat* of the nail gun could be heard everywhere in the house.

Annie knew she was blushing, but she hoped Olivia wouldn't notice. "It isn't nice to spy on people."

Straightening, Olivia advanced into the room and plopped down on the foot of Annie's bed. "I wasn't spying. I just happened to look out the window and see you two locking lips. You like him, don't you?"

The sweet memory of Shane's gentle kiss stole over Annie. Closing her eyes, she slipped back into the moment. The manly scent that was so uniquely his own, the way his lips had closed over hers with such tenderness, the feel of her heart beating like a drum inside her chest, the sound of his tiny sigh of regret when he pulled away.

"Yeah, I like him," she admitted.

"Is he a good kisser?"

"That's none of your business."

"Are you going to marry him?"

Shocked, Annie looked at Olivia in surprise. "What makes you ask that?"

"You're having his baby. It just seems like it would be a good idea to marry him."

"It would be a very bad idea."

"Why?" Raising her palm, she said, "No, don't tell me, let me guess. It's complicated."

"Yes, it is. Marriage isn't something to be taken lightly. Two people vow before God to spend the rest of their lives together. It's about acknowledging a profound love and respect for each other."

"So you don't love him?"

Not knowing exactly how to answer, she took her time and formed her words carefully. "I care about Shane, but two wrongs don't make a right. We barely know each other. If I were to marry him only for the sake of the baby, it's likely that we would both end up feeling trapped and unhappy. It might seem like the right thing to do, but in the long run it could be the worst thing for the two of us and especially for the baby. Do you understand?"

"Sort of. I guess it is complicated."

"Yes, it is, but since you're here, I meant to ask you what you thought about the meeting last night."

Olivia shrugged and picked at the frayed edge of her cutoffs. "I don't know."

"Was I too boring for words?"

Shaking her head, Olivia managed a half smile, "No, it wasn't that."

"Then what was it?"

"It was…sad. All those people had such terrible lives—even you and Pastor Hill. It doesn't seem fair. You're a nice person. Why did God do that to you?"

Reaching out, Annie tucked a lock of Olivia's dark hair behind her ear. "I did it to myself. I made bad choices over and over again. It took God and your mother to help me see that."

"Mom really does help people, doesn't she?"

"Yes, she really does."

Olivia looked down and tugged loose another string. "When you were in high school and drinking, did any of your friends care? I mean—could someone have helped you then?"

"Maybe, but no one tried."

"Wouldn't you have been mad if they told on you or something?"

"Probably, but I wish someone had."

Peering out from under her bangs, Olivia looked uncertain. "You do?"

"Of course I do. It would have meant that they really cared about me."

After a long pause, Olivia sighed. "I'm worried about my friend Heather."

"Why?"

"She's always talking about how cool it is that she gets drunk and her folks don't know."

"They know now. Shane told me that he spoke to her father that day at the base."

"She convinced them that it was her first time, only it wasn't, and she's been drinking since then."

"Have you been drinking, too?"

"Me? No way! Mom would ground me until I was a hundred if I ever did that again."

Smiling, Annie agreed. "At least that long. What do you think you should do about Heather?"

"I was hoping that you could talk to her. Only then she would know I squealed on her and she'd be mad at me."

"She might be mad, but if no one stops her, she's heading into a life of terrible pain. Have you talked to your mother about this?"

"No."

"Why not?"

"She's always so busy. Besides, she has enough to worry about."

"Olivia, your mother is never too busy to listen to you. She's a professional. She'll know what to do. I think it's very brave of you to try and help your friend."

"You do?"

"Absolutely."

Rising, Olivia started to leave but paused at the doorway and looked back. "Thanks, Annie."

"For what?"

"Just for stuff."

"You're welcome, kiddo."

"Hey, don't you have an appointment today?"

Startled, Annie glanced at the clock and jumped to her feet.

* * *

Shane entered the house just in time to see Annie come flying down the stairs.

"I'm ready," she said breathlessly. "I hope I haven't kept you waiting."

He stood speechless as she rushed past him to grab her purse from the coffee table. It was the first time he had seen her with her hair unbound. It spilled to her hips in a shiny, smooth cape that swayed as she walked.

"Thanks again for giving me a ride," she said.

"My pleasure," he muttered. He loved the way her hair seemed to capture and hold the light. The urge to reach out and touch it was overwhelming. It would be as soft and smooth as the finest silk.

Slinging her bag over her shoulder, she came and stood in front of him. Raising one eyebrow, she stared at him. "Well?"

He swallowed hard. "Well what?"

"Are you ready to go?"

"Sure." His feet felt rooted to the floor.

Pulling open her handbag, she withdrew a piece of colorful elastic fabric. Drawing her thick mane back with both hands, she deftly secured it at the nape of her neck. "Don't we have to actually leave the house?"

"For what?" He wished she would leave it loose.

"To go to the doctor's office," she said slowly and distinctly.

The word *doctor* brought him back to earth with a thump. "Oh, right. Sure."

He stepped back, allowing her to pass, and followed her out the door.

I'm a moron. How can I be mooning over her hair when she's pregnant with my baby?

The answer struck him as he watched her walk ahead of him to his car: he was falling in love with her.

She was a beautiful woman, but it was her inner beauty that was capturing his heart. If she cut off her hair and dyed it orange, he would still find her beautiful. He loved her strength and her determination. He loved the way she put her faith at the forefront of her life—even the way she stumbled and fell and got back up to face her mistakes. How could he ever be worthy of such a woman?

At his car, she tugged open the door and looked over her shoulder. "Is something wrong?"

Realizing that he was standing like a statue on the steps, he started toward her. "Nothing's wrong. I was distracted, that's all."

Did he dare tell her? He was sure that she liked him, but uncertainty held back the words. A year ago he had imagined himself in love with someone else. Someone who'd found it easy to leave him for another man.

Loath to risk that kind of pain again, he kept silent. Annie had made it plain from the start that she had her own life to live. Granting him the opportunity to stay involved with their child was a far cry from asking for a romantic relationship.

As he drove through the busy streets toward the clinic, he knew that he wouldn't say anything yet. Not until he was certain that Annie returned his feelings. If only his time with her wasn't so short.

Anything could happen while he was stationed in Germany. Annie could meet someone else.

"You need to turn right at the next corner," she said, pointing ahead.

"Thanks." He slowed the car.

"Shane, are you okay?"

He looked at her sharply. "Why do you ask?"

"You've been awfully quiet today."

"I'll try to talk it up on the way home."

"Are you nervous about coming to the doctor with me?"

"Now that you mention it—what if they don't have any good magazines in the waiting room?"

"They have a nice assortment. I'm sure you'll find something to interest you."

"Are you nervous?"

"No. I just hope I haven't gained too much weight. I hate getting on his scale. It weighs at least five pounds heavier than the one at home. Talk about depressing."

"You're no bigger than a minute. Why would you worry about your weight?"

"Okay, that was spoken like a man."

Pulling up beside the small redbrick structure with a blue-and-white medical symbol painted on the large plate-glass window, he parked the car. "Guys worry about important things."

"Like what?"

"Like is my hair getting thin? Or do these jeans make me look fat?"

"Ha-ha."

Annie pushed open her door and stepped out of the car. How was it that Shane could make her smile so easily? His company lightened her spirits and made her feel strangely happy. Could she trust the emotions he evoked? Were they real or only a matter of wishful thinking?

He joined her as she waited by the parking meter. She looked him up and down. His jeans were slightly dusty from his work on the roof and his blue T-shirt had seen better days, but to her eyes he looked tall, handsome and self-assured.

"They don't make you look fat at all, sweetie."

He half turned to look down at his hips. "You don't think so? Whew, that's a relief."

"I imagine your horse thinks the same thing when you dismount." She headed toward the building.

"Hey, that's not nice." He hurried to open the door for her.

"Ah, but is it true?" she threw over her shoulder as she walked past him.

Inside the building, the sounds of pop music came from a small television in the far corner of a long, narrow waiting room. The pale blue walls sported numerous posters with health information above the white plastic chairs that lined the perimeter. An elderly woman with a bandage on her hand glanced up as they came in, as did the two teenage girls in front of the TV. A harried mother holding a crying baby to her shoulder while a toddler tugged at the hem of her skirt paid them no attention at all.

Glancing at Shane, Annie said, "Why don't you have a seat?"

He nodded and made his way to an empty chair.

Annie crossed to the glass-fronted reception desk and spoke to the gray-haired woman seated behind it. "Hi, I'm

Annie Delmar and I'm here for an OB appointment with Dr. Merrick."

"Have you been seen here before?"

"Yes, back in March."

"I'll need you to fill out this paperwork and then have a seat."

"Can you tell me how long it will be?"

The woman pushed a clipboard toward her. "It'll take as long as it takes."

Accepting the paperwork and a pen, Annie made her way to a chair beside Shane. He leaned toward her and motioned toward the toddler, who had begun screaming at the top of his lungs. "Are you sure you want one of those?"

Annie stared at him in openmouthed astonishment. "Shame on you."

Looking contrite, he held up his hands. "Kidding. Just kidding."

"I hope so."

A nurse came into the room with a manila folder in her hands. "Belinda Kemp?"

"That's me." The woman with the baby herded the toddler in front of her as she followed the nurse down the hall.

Annie glared at Shane once more, then began filling out the forms the receptionist had given her. A short while later the same nurse came to the doorway and called her name.

The doctor, a man in his late fifties with a worn and haggard face, sat waiting for her. He didn't bother to look up when Annie was shown into the exam room. "Hello, Miss Delmar. How have you been feeling?"

"Good. The morning sickness is gone, and except for

feeling tired and a little swelling in my ankles, I'm doing okay."

"It looks like you're in your nineteenth week of pregnancy, is that right?"

"Yes."

"All right then, let's get started."

The exam itself didn't take long. After answering a barrage of questions, most of which she had already answered on paper, Annie was allowed to dress and waited as the doctor finished writing on the chart. She waited nervously for him to speak. Finally she asked, "Is everything okay?"

"As far as I can tell, it is, but I'd still like to get that sonogram just to make sure. Be sure to make that appointment next week and come in for a follow-up."

A stab of anxiety shot through Annie. "But I thought I wouldn't need to see you again for another month."

"I'd like to get the baseline sonogram and do some more lab work. Swelling in your feet this early concerns me a little, but your blood pressure is normal, so I'm not going to get excited about it. Limit your salt intake and put your feet up whenever you get the chance. I'm sure there's nothing to worry about. I'll see you in two weeks."

The doctor left the room and Annie stepped down from her seat on the exam table. Pressing a hand to her tummy, she tried to calm her apprehension. Dr. Merrick was taking precautions—that was all. The baby was fine. The sonogram would only confirm that.

She wished Shane were beside her instead of in the other room. She needed his arms around her and his voice telling her everything would be okay. In the next second, she decided not to tell him. She could worry enough for both of them.

Closing her eyes, Annie breathed a heartfelt prayer. *Please, Lord, don't let anything be wrong with my baby.*

Chapter Twelve

Thirty miles outside of Maddox, Kansas, Shane gazed forward between his mount's ears down the empty two-lane highway stretching away in the distance. The late-morning sun beat down on his shoulders, but he barely noticed. His mind was miles away—with Annie. He couldn't stop thinking about her.

It had only been two days, but it felt like weeks. If he missed her smile and her tart tongue this much after only forty-eight hours, what would it be like to be away from her for two years? The thought was depressing.

The creak of saddle leather, the sighing of the wind past his ears and the *clip-clop* of the horses' hooves were the only sounds. Until Avery opened his mouth again.

"I can't believe it. I can't believe you loaned your car to a woman. Are you nuts? What if she wrecks it? I don't know why you won't sell it to me. I've offered you more than it's worth several times."

Glancing over at his buddy riding beside him, Shane said, "Can we talk about something else?"

"Like what? The weather? It's hot." Avery pushed his cap back on his head. "It was hot an hour ago and it's still hot." Raising a hand to shade his eyes, Avery scanned the countryside. "Maybe you want to talk about the scenery. I see flat. It was flat an hour ago and it's still flat. If you look to your right, you will see miles of grass, but if you look quickly to your left, you will see—yes, that's right—miles of grass. How long is this ride going to be again?"

"One hundred miles."

"I was hoping I dreamed that part. One hundred miles divided by twenty-five miles a day. Are we really going to spend four days in the saddle?"

"It's not like we haven't been preparing for this." In fact, during the past month the unit had been riding all over the post and surrounding areas for up to six hours each day, conditioning both the men and the horses for this Memorial Day weekend event.

Eight men and their mounts moved along the verge of the road under a cloudless blue sky. Orange reflective vests worn for safety and the support vehicle following behind them were the only concessions the unit made to modern times. All the rest of the equipment was what any cavalry detachment in the 1860s would have carried.

Hoping to distract Avery from his sour mood, Shane asked, "Are you going to Lindsey and Brian's wedding next weekend?"

"I guess. What about you?"

"Yup, I told her I'd be there."

"Are you taking anyone?"

Frowning, Shane said, "I hadn't thought about it. Are you?"

"Certainly."

"Who?"

"There is a long line of women who would be delighted to spend the day with me. I just have to pick one."

Shaking his head, Shane said, "I don't think I've ever met someone who is so conceited with so little reason to be that way."

"Are you kidding? I'm a matrimonial prize of the first magnitude. All I have to do is mention that my grandfather is worth a fortune and women flock to me. They just don't need to know that I'm opposed to wedlock on a very visceral level."

The same wasn't true for Shane. Not since he'd met Annie. She had changed everything. The idea of spending his life with her had a deep appeal that settled into his chest and wouldn't be dislodged.

"What?" Avery demanded.

Drawn back to the conversation at hand, Shane said, "It doesn't seem right to string them along that way."

"I'm as sincere in my affection as they are—which is to say, only as deep as their pocketbooks."

Shane shook his head in disbelief at his friend's attitude. "You take the cake."

"Speaking of cake, I'm hungry."

"You'll get fed at the next town."

Rising in his stirrups, Avery shaded his eyes to look down the road. "There's nothing in sight yet."

"It gives a guy pause, doesn't it? Knowing that men like us rode this route as much as twice a week, escorting settlers westward, only a hundred and fifty years ago."

"The amazing part is that anyone stopped to settle in this place. They must have had a tree phobia."

A hundred yards ahead a white pickup rolled up to the highway and stopped beside a lone mailbox decorated with red, white and blue steamers. An elderly woman in a light blue skirt and a blue-and-white-flowered blouse got out of the truck and walked to the edge of the road. A man in a tan cowboy hat, red Western shirt and faded jeans joined her. She handed him a small American flag, then raised the one she held and waved it in the air.

Avery pulled his cap into place. Shane sat forward. All along the column riders straightened in their saddles. Even the horses lifted their heads and stepped higher.

"God bless you boys," she called out. "You make us proud."

At the front of the line Captain Watson turned aside and reined in. He touched the brim of his hat. "Thank you, ma'am."

Grinning, she stepped closer. "Our grandson is serving in the Middle East. He was so excited when I told him you'd be riding past our place. Would you mind if I took a picture?"

"I'd be delighted." Looking over his shoulder, he gave the order to halt. She pulled a camera from her white hand-bag and quickly snapped a half dozen shots.

Walking up, her husband took her arm. "That's enough, Lucy. They've got a long way to go."

She gave him an embarrassed smile. "Of course. Thank you for indulging a silly old woman, Captain."

"It was my honor."

"My husband's grandfather came west with the cavalry

in 1857 and settled here afterward. I think it's so special that the Army is recreating this part of our history after a century and a half."

Her husband nodded in agreement. "It's been the talk of the town for weeks now. Even some of the high school kids have been asking questions about what it was like in the old days."

"He's been telling and retelling his granddad's yarns to anyone who will listen."

"They're true stories, woman. Folks enjoy 'em."

"Almost as much as you enjoy yammering on. Captain, you and your men hurry along into Windom," Lucy said. "The ladies from our church are fixing lunch for all of you. You'll find fried chicken and homemade peach, cherry and pecan pies."

As the column began moving again, Avery leaned toward Shane. "This ride may have some highlights after all."

"Yeah, talking to people like that makes me proud of what we're doing." Would Annie be proud of him if she could see him now?

"I was thinking more about the food. I love pecan pie. And speaking of nuts—I can't believe you loaned your car to some woman. You must be in love."

Annie pulled the living room curtain aside and checked the street for the umpteenth time. Shane was due back today. It was ridiculous the way excitement zipped through her veins at the thought.

"This is silly." Dropping the folds of fabric, she crossed the room and picked up the remote. Aiming it at the television, she turned the set on. Forty channels later, she snapped it off again. Nothing held her interest. She glanced at the window and willed herself not to walk back there.

He had only been gone four days, but it seemed so much longer. Surely he would come by this evening to collect his car. Laying the remote down, she walked to the front door but stopped with one hand on the knob.

"This is absurd. Why am I a basket case?"

"Beats me," Crystal said, coming up behind her.

Feeling sheepish at being discovered talking to herself, Annie moved aside as Crystal pulled open the door. A tan sedan with gray primer on the right front fender pulled up to the curb behind Annie's blue hatchback. Shane's Mustang still sat in the driveway. Willie, dressed in a grimy white T-shirt with the sleeves cut out and baggy black pants, got out of the passenger side but stood at the curb without approaching the house.

Annie looked at Crystal in concern. "Are you going out again?"

"For a little while. Are you my mother now?"

Hurt by Crystal's sarcasm, Annie said, "I didn't mean to sound disapproving."

"You're just mad because Willie kept your car two days longer than he said he would. He explained that—he had to stay an extra day for a second job interview."

"He could have called to let us know. He's lucky I didn't report the car as stolen."

"Whatever. I'll see you later."

Annie reached out and took hold of her friend's arm, stopping her from leaving. "Crystal, I'm worried about you. You've been going out every night. You missed the last two AA meetings."

"So what? Do you think I'm drinking again? I'm not, so take a chill pill."

"I only want to help," Annie said softly.

Crystal's defiant attitude deflated. "I know. Don't worry. Willie is taking good care of me. He loves me. He's just going through a rough patch right now. His friend is driving us out to the lake for a couple of hours. Where's the harm in that? Trust me, okay?"

"I do. I just know how easy it is to get into a bad situation. Look at me. I'm the poster child for mistakes."

At the street, a military jeep pulled in behind the sedan. Shane stepped out of the passenger side. Bending down, he gave a brief wave to the driver. As the jeep pulled away, he straightened and began walking toward the house. Wearing jeans and the CGMCG's regulation red T-shirt that emphasized his muscular chest and flat abdomen, he looked wonderfully handsome. Annie's heart bounded into double-time.

As Shane walked past Willie, it was hard not to compare the two men. Shane's clean-cut, all-American physique contrasted sharply with Willie's slovenly dress and attitude.

Crystal's chin came up. "Your problem, Annie, is you can't stand to see people happy. You don't believe in love so you don't think anyone else should. Open your eyes. Grab a little joy before life passes you by. Happiness takes courage, too, you know."

Jerking her arm away, Crystal dashed down the walk and into Willie's embrace. After kissing him, she glanced back at Annie, then got in the car.

Pressing a hand to her throat, Annie watched them drive off. Something wasn't right with Crystal. As Shane came up to the bottom of the steps, his warm smile chased her worry about her friend from her mind. She said, "Welcome back."

"Thanks. Did you miss me?"

Oh, she had, but she wasn't about to admit it. "I certainly didn't miss the sound of your hammer on the roof."

"Will you miss the rain dripping in?"

"No, I won't miss that."

"Did you have any trouble with my car?"

"No. After Marge's quick refresher course on driving a manual transmission, I was able to manage."

"I'm glad."

"Thanks for letting me borrow your pride and joy. I know it must have been hard to leave it with me."

"You needed it more than I did."

She gestured toward the house. "Do you have time to come in? I just made a pitcher of lemonade, and Marge made some sugar cookies yesterday."

"That sounds great." The eagerness of his acceptance made her smile.

Happiness had been a rare thing in her life. She almost didn't recognize the emotion as it welled up inside her. Crystal was wrong. Annie wanted others to be happy— only she didn't expect it for herself. She hadn't done anything to deserve it. Feeling it now scared her witless.

Take a deep breath. Get a grip. It was good advice but hard to put into practice with Shane standing so close beside her. She took a step back. "How was your trip?"

"It was good. We met some wonderful people and I think we did some good PR for the Army."

He followed her into the house and into the kitchen. He

took a seat at the table, still talking about the reception the unit had received at various towns along their route. Annie pulled the lemonade pitcher from the refrigerator and filled two tall tumblers, glad of the chance it gave her to compose herself. By the time she placed one glass in front of Shane and set the platter of golden cookies sprinkled with red, white and blue sugar crystals on the table, she had herself well in hand.

"How have you been feeling?" Shane asked, then took a sip of his drink.

"A little tired and fat but otherwise good."

"You don't look fat at all. In fact, you look glowing."

"Thank you. Nice comeback. Who's been instructing you on how to talk to a pregnant woman?"

He managed to look sheepish and sweet at the same time. "I've been doing some reading."

Pleased beyond words that he cared enough to learn about the changes she was going through, Annie grinned and let the happiness seep back into her heart. He was a good man. She was doing the right thing by allowing him to be involved with the baby.

He set his glass down and ran his finger slowly around the rim. Sensing a change in his mood, she waited for him to speak. Had he changed his mind? Was he getting ready to give her and their child the brush-off?

Clearing his throat, he looked up and met her gaze with uncertainty in his eyes. "I know this is kind of short notice, but I was wondering if I could ask you for a favor?"

Puzzled, she said, "If I can. You've certainly done more than enough for me."

"Okay, that isn't exactly where I wanted to go with this. You don't owe me anything, so feel free to decline."

Waiting a full ten seconds for a further explanation, she finally said, "Spit it out."

"Do you remember Lindsey Mandel?"

"I'm not sure. Should I?"

"She gave the introduction for the Commanding General's Mounted Color Guard at the Community Appreciation Day."

"I think I remember her. She was a pretty woman with short, curly red hair?"

"That's her. She was a sergeant in my unit until she left the service back in April. Anyway, she's getting married this weekend and I was kind of wondering if you'd like to go with me to the wedding."

Annie blinked hard. "You want me to come to the wedding with you?"

"It won't be a big affair, but there is a reception after the ceremony. I'd like you to meet some of my friends." He looked braced for her refusal.

She opened her mouth to do just that but found herself remembering Crystal's words. *Grab a little joy before life passes you by. Happiness takes courage, too, you know.*

Had she been letting the joy of life pass her by? Did she have the courage to risk seeking a little happiness with Shane? He would be gone soon and she would be alone again. Knowing how badly she had dealt with such disappointments in the past made her afraid to risk it. She already cared for him far too much.

What do I do, Lord? Should I send him away and protect

what's left of my heart? Or do I say yes and gather a few more precious memories to treasure?

Either way, Annie knew heartache loomed in her future.

Chapter Thirteen

The chapel parking lot was nearly full when Shane pulled
in the following Saturday afternoon at a quarter till three.
Looking up, he saw the steeple over the bell tower of the
old stone building silhouetted against the fluffy white
clouds drifting past. Stepping out of his vehicle, he paused
to button the jacket of his dress uniform, then nervously
tugged it down and smoothed the front of the dark green
material. He wanted to look his best today.

The sound of organ music reached him coming through
the open panels of stained glass at the bottom of the arched
windows of the building. He walked around his newly
washed car and pulled open the passenger door. The vision
that took his hand and stepped out into the bright June
sunlight stole his breath.

Annie wore a simple pink dress with wide sleeves that
ended just above her elbows. Her long hair was held back
from her face by a band of matching material. Gathered
gently at a high waist, the drape of the supple fabric below
the vee neckline did little to hide her rounded tummy.

Beautiful, he decided, didn't do justice to her. His heart swelled with protectiveness and pride.

Taking her hand, he steered her toward the chapel doors.

Inside the cool interior, organ music played softly while they were escorted to the bride's side of the aisle. The scent of candles and carnations filled the air, and white bows adorned the ends of each row of wooden pews. After taking his seat beside Annie, Shane ran a finger under his collar to loosen his tie. Looking around, he recognized a dozen former and current members of the CGMCG. A few of them had wives or girlfriends beside them, but the majority of the young men had come alone, including Captain Watson, Avery and Lee.

Shane almost laughed when he caught Avery's eye. So much for the playboy's assumption that he could get a date at a moment's notice.

A few minutes later the organist fell silent. The minister, followed by Brian and two groomsmen, headed to their places in front of the altar. Brian leaned heavily on a cane, but when he looked toward the back of the church, his face lit up with happiness. Suddenly the first strains of the "Wedding March" rang out. All heads turned toward the end of the aisle.

Lindsey, dressed in a simple sleeveless ivory gown, stood with her hand resting on her father's sleeve. Standing with obvious military erectness, the gray-haired man's face beamed with a mixture of pride and sadness. As Lindsey started down the aisle, a shy smile curved her lips and love shone from her eyes as she gazed at the man waiting to make her his wife.

Shane looked down at the woman beside him. Lindsey made a radiant bride, but to his eyes she didn't hold a candle to Annie. Was he crazy to hope that Annie might someday look at him with the same kind of love in her eyes?

As the bride walked by, Annie watched with a touch of envy in her heart. Having given up the idea of a fairy-tale wedding a long time ago, it surprised her how much of that dream she still carried. To have her father walk her down the aisle, to stand in front of a church full of family and friends and pledge her heart to a very special man…what girl didn't want that?

Looking down, she brushed a hand over her bulging midriff. She had given up the right to that dream and so much more. It would be easy to blame the drinking, but the simple truth was that she had thrown away her dreams and destroyed whatever dreams her parents had held for her for a quick buzz. Having seen exactly how much a child could hurt a parent, Annie sent a quick prayer heavenward.

Please, gracious God, don't let my baby make the same mistakes I have made. I think I could face anything except watching her destroy herself.

As the music died away and the minister began to address the couple, Annie glanced at Shane and found him watching her with a look of such tenderness on his face that her heart melted. He made her want to believe in dreams again.

Had God forgiven her sins? Wasn't she asking for too much by even thinking about a life with a man as kind and loving as Shane? In spite of all the Lord had done for her, she still found it hard to accept the goodness in life. So many times she had been sure she'd found someone to make her happy, only to discover that so-called love was nothing more than an alcohol-induced illusion. Trusting her own judgment was sometimes hard. Trusting these new emotions was even harder. Was it love?

As if answering her unspoken question, the minister's words penetrated her mind. "Lindsey and Brian, I know that as a couple you are both in love with one another, but as wonderful as this feels, it is not a perfect love. With God's blessing, you will grow in loving and grow in spirit by loving one another.

"Love is patient. Love is kind. It is never jealous. Love does not brag. It is not arrogant. Love takes hard work. Sometimes love means you will have to suffer. But it is only through suffering that we discover our true strength. I pray that your relationship grows stronger, deeper and more beautiful as you face life's hardships and joys together until you find at last the true 'perfect love' with our Father in heaven."

Annie felt Shane take her hand. Meeting his gaze, she basked in the warmth of his smile. Love was patient. Love was kind. *Patient* and *kind* were exactly the words she would use to describe Shane, along with handsome and funny and more than a little determined. If she put her heart in his hands, he would treat it with tenderness and care. Brave or not, foolish or not, she would give herself one last chance at happiness.

When the ceremony came to an end, Annie and Shane followed the newlyweds and the crowd to the reception in a nearby hall. Surrounded by people she didn't know and unable to hide her condition, Annie had expected to feel awkward and out of place, but she soon discovered that Shane's friends were open and accepting. Keeping her hand tucked firmly against his side, Shane moved from group to group introducing her, regaling her with stories about the men he served with and making her feel at ease.

When the bride and groom approached, Shane pulled Annie close and slipped his arm around her waist.

Nestled against his waist, Annie struggled to contain the joy leaping like a fountain in her chest. She smiled at the bride. "The ceremony was beautiful and you look lovely."

"Thank you. I'm so glad you could come today, Annie. Shane has told us so much about you."

"Has he?" Slanting a glance up at him, Annie thought she detected a faint blush creeping up his cheeks.

"I might have mentioned you a time or two," he admitted. "It was all good."

"I doubt that."

"Okay, it was mostly good. I can't help it that you're stubborn and contrary, as well as gorgeous."

"The gorgeous part was a good touch. Keep that up and I'll have to start liking you."

"So flattery is all it takes to get on your good side? I wish I had known that sooner."

"What makes you think you're on my good side?"

Lindsey laughed. "I see you are a woman after my own heart. Keep him in line, dear. Please excuse us. I believe it's time for us to cut the cake. Come on, Brian, your surgical skill with a knife will come in handy with this."

As they walked away, Shane grinned at Annie. "Are you having a good time?"

Happier than she could remember being in a long time, she smiled at him and nodded. "I am. Thank you for bringing me."

Shane battled the urge to kiss Annie there in front of everyone. He knew it would embarrass her, but the sight of her sweet lips parted in a smile just for him was almost too much to bear. Suddenly her eyes widened and she pressed a hand to her stomach.

"What is it? What's wrong?" he asked in concern.

"Nothing's wrong. Someone is just kicking me."

"Really? May I feel it?"

"You can try. It's very faint." Taking his hand, she pressed it against her belly.

Shane thought he detected the tiniest tap beneath his palm, but he couldn't be sure.

"Wow, did you feel that?" Annie asked.

His son or daughter had kicked his hand! There was a real baby, his baby, nestled under the heart of this beautiful and brave woman.

A sense of profound wonder and delight poured into his heart, followed quickly by gut-wrenching panic. With painful certainty, Shane realized he had absolutely no idea how to be a father.

God, I know You and I are just getting acquainted, but You've got to help me. Please don't let me mess this up.

"Yeah, I felt it," he admitted weakly.

She frowned. "Are you okay?"

He met her worried eyes. "I've been talking about having a son or a daughter for weeks, but until this minute it wasn't real."

Another faint thump-thump fluttered against his fingers, causing a slow grin to spread across his face. "That's some kid we've got there. Does he do this all the time?"

"*She* does it a few dozen times a day."

"It feels so weird."

"You're telling me. You should feel it from the inside."

"It must be a boy. With that kind of kick, he's sure to be a soccer forward."

"Girls play soccer, too."

"My little girl is going to play house with her dolls and have tea parties. She isn't going to be a jock."

"I know your detachment reenacts things from a bygone era, but you are going to have to come back to the present, buddy. Girls can play house *and* soccer."

"All kidding aside, Annie, it doesn't make a bit of difference to me if it's a boy or a girl. I just want the two of you to be healthy."

"We are. Don't worry."

Reaching out, he brushed back a strand of her hair and let his hand cup her cheek. "That's the funny part—I can't help but worry. You have become very important to me, Annie."

She covered his hand with her own. "I feel the same way about you."

"You do?"

Grinning, she said, "Don't sound so surprised."

"I'm not—I mean, I'd hoped, but I wasn't sure."

"I wasn't sure myself until today."

"I hope you know how special you are and how happy I am whenever we're together. You've changed my life in so many ways. I want to spend every minute I can with you, Annie. I think we have something good going on."

"Really?" The shy uncertainty in her tone touched his heart.

"Really."

Looking down, she said, "Because of the baby."

With one finger beneath her chin, he lifted her face until she met his eyes. "Not because of the baby."

His transfer back to the First Infantry Division and his deployment to Germany loomed like a dark cloud over his delight in knowing Annie returned his feelings. There was so little time left for them to be together.

"Look, the color guard is leaving again early Tuesday morning, and we'll be gone another week. Maybe we could spend the day together tomorrow?"

Her smile faded. "I'd love to, but I have to work."

"Okay, what about Monday? I could get away for a few hours in the afternoon, but I'd have to be back at four. It's my turn to have the duty."

"I work until one. After that, I have a doctor's visit scheduled at two o'clock."

He tried not to sound disappointed. "Then we'll make time after I get back from our tour in Missouri."

Annie bit her bottom lip, then raised her chin. "If you want, you could come with me to my doctor's appointment and maybe stay for the sonogram. That way we could both see our soccer player's first photos."

"Do you mean it? Of course I'll come with you."

"You will?"

"Wild horses couldn't keep me away." Shane knew he was grinning like a fool, but he couldn't help it.

"I'll have to take your word for that since you're the horse-and-mule expert."

Someday he would tell her how much he adored the twinkle in her eyes when she teased him. He needed a distraction—fast—or he was going to have to kiss her.

As if she were reading his thoughts, she took a step to his side. "I think they've finished cutting the cake."

"Are you hungry?"

"I'm five months pregnant. I'm always hungry."

"Then I'll go get some for both of us."

"Don't forget the mints," she called after him.

Shane headed toward the linen-draped side table where several women were dishing up slices of white wedding cake onto clear plastic dishes. After requesting an extra-large slice and extra mints for one of his plates, Shane turned around to see Annie engaged in animated conversation with another young woman who was also obviously pregnant.

He stood for a moment, drinking in the sight of her. He loved the way she touched the roundness of her stomach with such tenderness. He loved the way she smiled at him from across the room. God had given him Annie and a child. He couldn't imagine feeling happier.

Two days after the wedding, Annie lay on the hard exam table at the clinic with only her bulging tummy exposed for her first sonogram. She was more excited than worried. After all, the baby was moving all the time now and Dr. Merrick had assured Annie that this was merely a precaution. The speckled ceiling tiles overhead were decorated with several colorful posters of babies sleeping in giant flowers. They were cute, but Annie was much more interested in the small black-and-white image wavering on the sonogram screen.

Shane, looking nervous, sat by Annie's side and held her hand.

The sonogram technician, dressed in pink scrubs with blue baby footprints scattered across her top, chatted constantly as she readied her equipment. "My name is Becky and I'm going to be doing your sono. Is this your first child?"

"Yes," Shane answered before Annie could, then sent her a sheepish grin. It was clear he was excited about the prospect of seeing his son or daughter on the machine's small screen.

"It's my first pregnancy, too," Annie replied, giving his hand a squeeze.

"All right, I'm going to put some gel on your stomach and it's going to be cold," Becky warned.

Cold and icky, Annie would have said. Static crackled as the wand made contact with Annie's skin.

"How far along are you?" Becky asked, typing on the keyboard of the machine.

"I'll be exactly twenty-one weeks tomorrow."

Becky arched an eyebrow as she looked at Annie. "You sound positive about that."

"We are," Annie and Shane said simultaneously, then grinned at each other.

"What are we looking at?" Shane asked.

"The lunar landing?" Annie suggested, turning her head slightly. She certainly couldn't make a baby out of the streaky image. Suddenly a rapid, faint knocking sound came out of the speakers.

"Is that her heartbeat?" The awe in Shane's tone made Annie's heart turn over. His grip on her hand tightened.

"Yes, it is," Becky said.

"Why is it so fast?" he asked.

"Babies normally have a heart rate of one-twenty to one-sixty beats a minute. Girls run slightly higher than boys. Your little one has a pulse of about one-eighty. That's a little fast, but maybe he or she is just excited to be on TV."

Annie lifted her head to see the screen better. "Does that mean it's a girl?"

"We'll get to that question in a few minutes if you want to find out, but first I have a few measurements to check. Ah, I see a foot." Becky pointed to the center of the screen, where the wavering gray image took shape.

"I see it." Shane moved closer, his voice brimming with pride and exhilaration.

Her baby's foot. Annie couldn't find the words to describe the feeling coursing through her. A second later it hit her. This was love—overwhelming in its intensity—and it took her breath away. She met Shane's gaze and saw the same raw emotion on his face.

Their child—conceived with utter carelessness— brought a joy more powerful than anything Annie had known in her life.

As Becky moved the wand over Annie's stomach, she kept up a running conversation about what she was doing and pointed out various parts of the baby's anatomy. Annie listened with only half an ear. The rest of her was tuned in to the sound of her baby's heartbeat.

Closing her eyes, she thanked God for the blessing He had given her. It was one she didn't deserve. It took several long minutes before Annie noticed that Becky had fallen silent.

Glancing at the young woman's face, Annie felt her heart freeze, then begin to pound with painful intensity. "What's wrong?"

Pressing the wand more firmly into Annie's stomach, Becky avoided looking at her. "I just need to get a few more pictures of something here."

"Everything is okay, isn't it?" Shane asked.

Becky chewed her lower lip, then said, "I'm having a little trouble getting the measurements I need. I'm going to have Dr. Merrick give it a try. He's better at this than I am."

Annie didn't believe her. Looking at Shane, she saw he didn't, either. And she saw something else. She saw fear in his eyes. Her heart sank as panic welled up like bile in her throat and threatened to choke her.

Chapter Fourteen

"It's going to be okay," Shane said quietly.

Sitting in a chair beside him in Dr. Merrick's office, Annie desperately wanted to believe Shane, but she couldn't. Trying to think about anything but what could be wrong, she glanced around the room. The small office contained only a desk with a computer and two gray filing cabinets sitting side by side against the wall. Over them hung several framed documents detailing Dr. Merrick's credentials. On the other wall hung several photographs of a little boy and a little girl.

Annie rubbed her hands up and down her arms. "What's taking him so long?"

"I wish I knew." Shane's knuckles stood out white as he gripped the arms of the chair. Annie's hands were ice-cold. She struggled to keep her composure. This couldn't be happening. Her baby was going to be fine.

God, why are You doing this to me? I'm sorry for all the things I've done wrong, You know that. Please let my baby be okay.

The office door opened and Dr. Merrick came in at last. "I'm sorry to keep you waiting, but I wanted to get a second opinion on what your sonogram was showing us and do a little research."

He sat down at his desk and faced them. "I've sent a digital copy of your sonogram to a colleague at Children's Mercy in Kansas City, and unfortunately he concurs with my diagnosis."

"What's wrong?" Annie asked the question, but she knew in her heart she didn't want to hear the answer.

Dr. Merrick folded his hands together. "There isn't an easy way to say this. Your child has a rare condition called congenital cystic adenomatoid malformation. We call it C-CAM for short. It is a birth defect that occurs when one or more lobes of the lungs develop into fluid-filled cysts instead of normal tissue. The result is that your baby has a large tumor inside her chest, and it's growing."

"It's a girl?" The thrill of knowing she carried a daughter couldn't offset the dread filling her mind.

"This tumor is treatable, isn't it?" Shane asked.

Hearing the desperation in his voice, Annie bowed her head and fought to keep from screaming. This couldn't be happening. She wanted to wake up from this horrible nightmare.

Please, God, let me wake up!

"Treatment depends on the size of the tumor. Many small ones don't require intervention, but in this case we can already see that the baby's heart is being compressed to the point that it isn't pumping blood adequately. With a tumor this size, the child can't survive."

"No!" The cry tore out of Annie throat. "Don't say that! There's some mistake!"

Shane reached over to take her hand, but she jerked away from him.

The doctor said, "I wish that were true. I'm very sorry. This isn't an inherited condition. You don't need to worry about it reoccurring with your next pregnancy."

"But I want *this* baby," Annie whispered. "Can't you help us?"

The man's silence spoke louder than any words. Annie's throat closed up, and tears poured unchecked down her face as the terrible truth sank in.

Shane's heart ached for Annie's pain. She seemed to shrink into a ball of agony before his eyes. He wanted to comfort her, but he didn't know how. The knowledge that their daughter was going to die numbed his mind.

None of his military training had taught him how to deal with such grief. He looked back at the doctor. "Is there any chance at all that the baby can survive?"

"I don't want to give you false hope. In a very few cases the cysts stop growing and the baby can survive until it is mature enough to be born and undergo surgery to remove the tumor. It isn't likely in this case because we can already see signs of heart failure in the fetus."

"But there is a chance?" Shane snatched onto that thread of hope with grim determination.

"I'll recheck a sonogram in a few days. That will tell us for sure if the tumor is still growing. The only other option would be fetal surgery. You'd have to go to a specialized center for that. I think the closest one would be Houston, but the baby may already be too sick."

Shane glanced at Annie. She sat silent in her chair, her head bowed in defeat. "This fetal surgery—it's been done in cases like this?"

"A very few, and not all have been successful."

"And we can have it done in Houston?"

"Among other places. But, Mr. Ross, there are other things to consider. Fetal surgery is risky for the mother. Many times the babies die anyway. Even if it is successful, Annie would need to stay in the hospital for weeks to be monitored for premature labor. She has no insurance, she has a minimum-wage job. You yourself are being deployed overseas in a few weeks and won't be there to support her."

"You don't know how strong Annie is," Shane said.

"I'm afraid I can't recommend fetal surgery as a course of treatment. I see from your records that this wasn't a planned pregnancy and that you two aren't married. An unwanted pregnancy places a terrible strain on a couple at the best of times. I see men and women trying to cope and failing all the time. They suffer and their children suffer. Doing nothing and letting nature take its course may be the best thing for both of you."

Annie's voice quivered as she asked, "Did I cause this? We were drinking the night I conceived. Is that the reason this happened?"

Shaking his head, Dr. Merrick said, "We don't know why these things happen. I'm sorry, Annie. This may sound cruel, but given your history of alcoholism, this may be a blessing in disguise. In time, you can continue to make a better life for yourself without the added burden of an un-planned pregnancy."

On a practical level what the physician said made sense, but Shane's heart wouldn't allow him to stand by and lose the very reason his life had taken on a new meaning. Annie and the baby were everything to him. God had given him a gift unlike anything he had ever expected or deserved. He couldn't—wouldn't—give up without a fight.

"We want you to find a specialist in Houston to see us," he insisted.

"Don't you think Annie is the one who should make that decision?"

Annie smoothed her hands over her stomach. "How will it happen? I mean, what can I expect? How will I know when the baby is…"

Dr. Merrick sat back in his chair. "Sometime soon, the baby will stop moving. Once that happens, labor should begin in a few days. If it doesn't, we can induce labor with drugs and deliver the fetus that way."

Annie sprang to her feet. "I can't…I'm sorry." With one hand pressed to her lips, she hurried out of the room.

Rising, Shane started to follow her, but Dr. Merrick stopped him by saying, "Give her a little time alone. I know this has been a shock to both of you."

Shock didn't begin to cover the emotions he was going through. It had to be so much worse for Annie. If he hadn't been so self-centered and thoughtless the night he met her, none of this would be happening. There had to be a way to save his child. "I want you to find a doctor in Houston that we can see."

"Very well, I'll see about a referral, but I think you're only looking at more heartache if you get your hopes up."

"Maybe, but I need to know I've done everything I can."

"Leave your phone number with my receptionist and I'll give you a call as soon as I hear something."

"Thank you."

After leaving the small office, Shane gave his number to the woman at the desk and went looking for Annie. He found her leaning against the hood of his car, looking lost and forlorn as she wiped away her tears with the back of her hand.

He enveloped her in a hug, holding her close and trying to offer some comfort. She stiffened in his embrace and turned her face away. "Take me home, please."

Shane pulled back but kept his hands on her shoulders. Lowering his face to try and meet her eyes, he said, "Dr. Merrick is going to find a surgeon in Houston for us."

She wouldn't look at him. "Just take me home."

"Annie, please. Don't give up."

"God is punishing us. We sinned and He is taking my baby away because of it."

"You don't believe that."

She looked at him then. Her eyes were dull and devoid of hope. "Yes, I do. I've led a terrible life. I should never have expected to get off scot-free. I'm sorry now that I told you about the baby. I should have kept my mouth shut. If I had, you wouldn't be suffering, too. I can't get it right. No matter how hard I try, I can't make good decisions."

"Don't blame yourself for this."

"Take me home." Her words were barely audible.

"I'm angry at God, too. You don't deserve this. Our

baby doesn't deserve this, but I don't believe God would punish an innocent child for our indiscretions."

"Why couldn't God take me instead?" Her voice was little more than a whisper. "Why? Why let me love this baby and then steal it back? Our baby is going to die, Shane. Nothing else matters. Nothing."

He could feel Annie retreating further and further away from him, and he didn't know how to counter it. Sick with grief and rising fear, he shook her shoulders. "Listen to me, Annie. We're not going to give up without a fight."

"I can't fight. Not anymore. Not this, too. Let go of me. I'll walk home."

She tried to pull away from him, but he held on. "No, I'll drive you."

Perhaps talking to Marge would help Annie regain her perspective. He opened the car door. Annie hesitated but then got in. Moving around to the driver's side, Shane got in, as well. Starting the Mustang, he managed to make the drive to Annie's home, although when he pulled up at the curb he wasn't certain exactly how he had gotten there.

After pulling his key from the ignition, he paused with his hands on the wheel. Annie started to get out, but he stopped her by taking hold of her arm. "I know you're hurting, Annie. I'm hurting, too, so don't shut me out. I love you. We'll get through this together."

Annie recognized the numbness enclosing her. In some tiny corner of her mind she knew that when it wore off, the pain would be unbearable. There was only one way to keep the pain at bay. She had lived in an emotionless fog for years. Drinking would keep her numb.

Who would blame her? God had betrayed her. What could He do that was worse than what He had already done?

He could take Shane away, too.

All her hopes and daydreams of a life with Shane turned to ashes on her tongue. The baby would die soon. Just thinking the words shredded her soul.

Shane would leave for Germany in a few weeks. Without the baby to hold him, there would be no reason for him to come back. She'd be alone again with no one to care if she lived or died. No one to love and be loved by.

It's not fair!

She wanted to scream it to the heavens. It was bad enough that God was making her wait and watch as her child perished. She couldn't stand the thought of waiting and watching Shane's love wither, too. A clean break would be less painful for both of them.

"We aren't together, Shane. You wanted to be included in your baby's life. Now there isn't going to be a baby, so you can stop pretending I matter."

He reached out and turned her face toward his. "Of course you matter to me. I haven't been pretending. I love you, Annie."

"Then I guess I've been the one pretending." Her voice broke, but she didn't care as she pulled out of his grasp.

"Don't do this," he begged. "Don't push me away."

"I'll let you know…when…when it's over. Until then, please leave me alone." Pushing open the door, she got out and hurried into the house as a new round of tears began to fall.

Chapter Fifteen

Shane paced the small space in front of Pastor Hill's untidy desk. "Annie won't see me. I've been back to the house twice today. Marge says she has locked herself in her room and she won't come out. I'm really worried about her."

"Hearing such terrible news must have been very difficult for both of you."

"She blames God."

"That's not the least bit surprising. God's shoulders are broad. He understands grief. He watched His own son die a cruel death on the cross."

"I know. I'm trying to accept this. I'm trying to understand that it's His will, but part of me can't. I want to do something. Anything."

"That would be the human part of you, Shane. Do what you can and trust that God's love is there to comfort you no matter what the outcome."

"It's hard."

"For a man so new to this faith, I'd say you're doing remarkably well."

"Annie showed me the way. I don't think I would have gone looking for God if it hadn't been for her."

The sudden ringing of his cell phone startled Shane. He yanked it from his pocket, only to lose his grip on it. He juggled it in midair a few times before he regained his hold and snapped it open. "Ross here."

"Corporal Ross, this is Dr. Merrick."

"Yes, Doctor."

"I've managed to contact a surgeon in Houston who is willing to see Annie and evaluate her for surgery."

"That's great."

"You'll need to get her there as soon a possible. I would strongly advise against driving that distance. An air ambulance would be the safest and fastest way to get her there. I have the number of a service in Kansas City if you are interested. I'm afraid the cost will be about five thousand dollars up front, as Annie has no insurance. Will that be a problem?"

Shane's heart sank. Coming up with five thousand dollars quickly wouldn't be easy. He was certain Annie didn't have that kind of cash lying around, and neither did he. Even if he could manage the financial part, would Annie accept his help?

"Thanks for all you've done, Dr. Merrick."

"You're welcome. I wish you the best."

After writing down the air-transport service's number and the contact information of the doctor waiting for them in Houston, Shane snapped his phone shut and dialed Marge's number.

Olivia picked up on the second ring. "Hello."

"Olivia, this is Shane. Can I speak to Annie?"

"I'm not sure she'll talk to you, but I'll try."

"Good girl." He waited impatiently as Olivia laid down the phone. After several long minutes she came back on the line.

"She won't talk to me, but she let Crystal in the room."

"That's good. At least she's talking to someone. Is your mother home?"

"She had to go back to work for a little bit, to get someone to cover for her. She said she'd be back as soon as she could."

"All right, give Annie this message even if you have to yell it though the door. Tell her that I'm taking her to Houston tonight."

"How are you going to do that?"

"I'm not sure, but I'll pick up a crowbar on the way in case I have to break into her room."

"Mom isn't going to like that."

He had to chuckle. *Please, God, give me the chance to raise a daughter as adorable as Marge's.*

"I'm kidding, Olivia. I'll be there as soon as I take care of a couple of things."

He hung up the phone and turned to Pastor Hill. "Keep us in your prayers, Pastor."

"That goes without saying. Annie is a dear friend. She has suffered so much in her young life. Don't blame her for retreating from you. Experience has taught her to expect the worst from life. But did I hear you say you were going with her? Can you get emergency leave from the Army by tonight?"

"I'll do what I have to do. My daughter is going to get her chance at life even if I get court-martialed for doing it."

Annie lay curled on her side in her bed. Her pillow was damp from the tears she had shed. Tears that brought no relief from the pain in her heart. Through puffy eyes, Annie gazed out the window. The glass framed the top of the maple in the backyard and the dark clouds moving in from the west. The occasional flash of lightning in the distance warned of the storm's approach. Annie shivered and rolled over.

Crystal sat on the twin bed next to her. For the past half hour she had listened to Annie's story without saying much.

"I wanted this baby, Crystal. Maybe not at first, but later I did. I wanted someone to need me and love me."

Crystal stroked Annie's hair away from her face. "I'm really sorry, Annie. Life ain't fair."

"Why is God doing this to me?"

"If you ask me, God doesn't much care about the likes of us."

"I thought He did. I thought He loved me. Pastor Hill and Marge both talk about God's unconditional love, and I believed them. I don't know what to think now. I want this whole thing to be some terrible mistake."

"I wish I could help."

"No one can help. I haven't felt her move since I left the doctor's office today. That was hours ago. What if she's already…dead? How do I know? I can't bear to think about waiting for it to happen."

"I'm sorry, but the doctor may have been right about one

thing—you don't need a kid messing up your life. I tried to tell you that, but you wouldn't listen."

"I want to forget everything. I want to forget that I loved my baby and that I loved Shane. I don't want to go through this. Please, someone help me."

"If you really want to forget things, I can help with that." Crystal rose from the bed and dropped to her hands and knees. From beneath her mattress she pulled out a bottle of vodka. Standing once more, she held it out to Annie. "You need this more than I do."

"You started drinking again? Oh, Crystal, I knew Willie was bad news for you."

"I have things I want to forget, too, Annie. A lot of things. Willie understands that. He doesn't think it's wrong. He doesn't judge me the way others do. He loves me. Besides, don't tell me you don't want a drink right this minute. I know the signs. What's it going to hurt? Not your baby anymore."

Crystal tossed the bottle onto the bed beside Annie. As fascinating and as deadly as any viper, Annie couldn't take her eyes off it. It would be so easy to take one sip and then another and another. Soon she would forget everything as it numbed the terrible pain gnawing in her chest. It would be so easy.

Except it would harm the baby. If she were still alive. Was she suffering? Would alcohol numb her little one's pain the way it numbed hers?

Don't think like that. But once the idea had planted itself in her brain, it wouldn't leave.

"I don't want it," Annie said, pushing the bottle away.

Oh, but she did. Anything to take away the pain in her heart and blot out this terrible day.

"Sure you do. I know I need one for the road." Crystal turned, moved to the closet and pulled out a worn black suitcase. She swung it up onto her twin bed and unzipped it.

Annie tore her gaze away from the bottle. "What are you doing?"

"I'm moving in with Willie." After scooping an armful of clothes from the dresser in the corner, Crystal dumped them in the bag, then turned back to the closet.

"Crystal, don't. Think about what you're doing."

Tossing dresses, hangers and all, onto her bed, she held up one final piece, a red tank top with a blue beaded flower on the front. "Is this one yours or mine? I forget."

"It's yours."

"Good." Tossing it toward the suitcase, Crystal then picked up three pairs of shoes from the closet floor. After stuffing them into the back corner of the bag, she closed the lid and leaned on it to zip it shut.

"Crystal, don't go. How can I go through this without you?"

Hefting the case, Crystal walked to the door. Annie rose and grabbed her arm. "Don't make me lose my best friend and my baby on the same day."

"I'm no good in a crisis, Annie. I never was. I'm really sorry about the baby, but there's nothing I can do to help. I'll be in touch. Keep the bottle. Willie will buy me another one."

Crystal unlocked the door, pulled it open and stepped out into the hall. Annie followed her. At the top of the stairs Crystal turned back and said, "Shane is downstairs. Do you want to see him?"

Clutching her head with her hands, Annie tried to think. She couldn't face Shane. She couldn't face anyone. "No. Tell him to go away."

Annie stepped back into her room and slammed the door shut. Turning the button on the knob, she made sure it was locked, then she leaned her head against the wood panel and hoped that Shane would go away.

Shane stepped aside as Crystal came down the stairs. She said, "Annie doesn't want to see you. This is your fault, you know."

"Where are you going?" Olivia asked from the sofa.

Crystal touched her eyebrows with her index finger. "I've had it up to here with God and AA. I'm leaving. Tell your mom thanks for everything."

Olivia shot to her feet. "But you can't go. Annie needs us. Tell her, Shane."

Crystal looked down and wouldn't meet his eyes.

He said, "If she wants to leave, we can't stop her. Someday she'll realize what a mistake she is making."

Turning his back on her, he walked up the stairs. Annie was the important one. At the top, he heard the front door closing, but he didn't pause. He approached Annie's door and took a deep breath. Raising his fist, he knocked softly. "Annie, it's Shane. Please let me in."

Silence was the only reply.

He tried a more forceful tone. "Annie, open this door."

"Go away! Go away! Why won't you leave me alone?"

"Because I love you. Please let me in." He tried the

knob, but it was locked. The door and the jamb looked like solid oak. He wasn't sure he could break it down. Even if he tried, Annie might be standing on the other side. He couldn't risk hurting her by barreling through the door.

"Okay, Annie, you win for now." Again only silence answered him. He turned and hurried down the stairs. At the bottom, he turned into the kitchen. Olivia was close behind him.

"Where are you going? Is Annie okay?"

Recognizing the worry in Olivia's voice, he stopped and took her by the shoulders. "Annie will be fine."

"There's a storm coming. She's afraid of storms."

"I'm going to take care of her."

"Is it true the baby is dead?"

"We don't know that for sure. I'm taking Annie to see a doctor who can help save the baby." He pulled a card from his pocket. "I need you to give this to your mother when she gets back if we are gone by then. You're being really brave, Olivia."

"You are *so* wrong. I'm scared out of my mind!"

He pulled her close in a quick hug. "I'm sorry, kid."

"That's okay. Just go save the day. That's what the cavalry does, isn't it?"

He leaned back to grin at her. "That's the plan."

"What can I do?"

"I want you to run out and tell the taxi driver to keep waiting. I don't care how much it costs. Then I want you to go up and keep talking to Annie. Let her know she isn't alone."

"She tried to kill herself a long time ago. Do you think she might do something like that again?"

He drew Olivia close in a tight hug as he glanced at the ceiling. "Annie is so much stronger than she realizes. We just need to make her see that. Now, go on and don't stop talking until her door opens."

Olivia nodded and hurried to the front door. Shane went out the back.

Annie heard Shane leave, but instead of relief, all she felt was betrayal. God, Crystal and now Shane. They had all deserted her.

A cold anger replaced her grief. She had been foolish and naive to count on any of them. Turning back to her bed, she saw the bottle lying among the folds of her pink-and-white-patchwork quilt. There was one thing she knew she could count on.

Walking to the foot of her bed, she picked it up and held the cool glass to her chest. Was there enough to dull the pain? Enough to send her into oblivion? Slowly she unscrewed the cap.

The sound of Olivia's voice outside her door made her look up, and she caught sight of herself in the mirror over the dresser. Blinking hard, she took a good, long look. She saw a pathetic woman clutching a bottle of booze like a treasure above her pregnant stomach.

Shane had told Dr. Merrick that she was a strong woman. Shane didn't know the woman she had been. He didn't know the woman in the mirror.

Suddenly her anger came roaring to the forefront. "What do you want from me, God? Tell me what You want and I'll do it," she yelled. "I'll do anything except go back to what I was. I won't do that!" She threw the bottle at the mirror and they both broke into pieces.

A strange calm filled her mind, then a tiny flutter stirred under her heart. Relief made her knees weak. Her daughter still lived.

She took a step back and sat on the edge of the bed. Closing her eyes, she breathed a prayer of thanks.

She would treasure each moment, each quivering movement until the very end. If this was all the time she had left with her baby, she was going to spend it with the utmost care.

Sounds made her look up and she saw Shane stepping into her room through the window. The oddity of it didn't even strike her as strange. Smiling at him, she said, "The baby moved. She isn't gone."

He crossed the room and dropped to his knees beside her. "Thank God."

"I'm sorry I tried to keep you away. She's your child, too. I see how wrong I was."

"Are you okay?"

"I almost took a drink. I wanted to so badly."

"But you didn't."

She reached out and cupped his cheek. "No. Thank you for believing in me."

Covering her hand with his own, he turned his face to kiss her palm. "I believe in us." Rising to his feet, he said, "I have an air ambulance on its way to the airfield. There is a surgeon in Houston who will meet us at the hospital and tell us if he can help the baby."

"Oh, Shane, I don't know if I can do it. What if we get

our hopes up only to hear that she can't be saved. Right now she is with us, surrounded by the people who love her."

"Annie, you're right, we both love her. No matter what happens, that love won't change. She is in God's hands. She always has been. If He takes her from us, it will be to carry her to a place of perfect peace."

"I know, but I want her here with me."

"So do I. I don't know what God has planned for us, but if there is even a remote chance that our baby might live, we have to try. We will do everything humanly possible and leave the rest up to God. Do you remember when I told you my father wasn't involved when I grew up?"

"Yes. I remember thinking how sad you looked when you said it."

"That wasn't the whole truth. My father lived in the same town as my mother and I did. He had a nice house and a successful business, while we lived in a run-down rented trailer. He also had a wife and three kids. Not once in my life did he acknowledge me."

"Oh, Shane." Her heart ached for the little boy he had been and the pain he had endured.

"When my mother died, he came to the funeral. I was so scared and worried about what would happen to me. I saw him, I thought he had come to take me home with him. I didn't have anyone else. But he left without even speaking to me. Do you know how unwanted, how unloved that made me feel?"

"I'm so sorry he hurt you."

"I vowed that day that I would never be anything like him."

"You aren't."

"That's why I can't stand by and do nothing. My baby has to know that I will turn the world upside down for her."

"I understand, but I'm afraid…afraid to start hoping again."

"I'll be with you, Annie. Together we can face the worst, because we have faith that it isn't the end."

She stared into his eyes, their bright blue depths full of pleading. Finally she nodded. "All right. I'll go."

He pulled her to her feet and into his arms. "That's my brave Annie. Come on, we have a plane to catch."

Sniffling, Annie wiped her eyes. "If I'm going to be staying in Houston until she's born, I'll need a few things."

"Okay, but hurry. I've got a taxi waiting outside."

He opened the bedroom door. Olivia sat on the floor outside. Rising to her feet, she frowned at him and said, "How did you get in?"

"I used the ladder from the garden shed to get up on the roof and then I came in through the window."

"Cool. You Army guys rock."

Annie hurried to the closet but paused with her hand on the doorknob. Looking over her shoulder at Shane, she said, "Crystal left. She's drinking again."

"I know."

"I was too wrapped up in my own problems to see that she needed help."

"It's not your fault."

"I know that. She will have to find her own way back. I pray she does. Olivia, will you help me pack?"

In a few minutes Annie had the necessities gathered and stuffed into her threadbare green duffel bag. Shane picked it up and held open the bedroom door to let Annie and Olivia precede him. Annie was halfway down the stairs when a loud clap of thunder shook the house.

Irrational panic stole her breath. She collapsed onto the steps and covered her ears with her hands.

Chapter Sixteen

"Annie, what is it?" Shane dropped the duffel bag on the steps and made his way to her side. She didn't answer him.

At the bottom of the stairs Olivia turned around. "It's the storm. She's petrified of them."

Shane pulled Annie's hands away from her face. "Annie, listen to me. We need to go. It's just a storm."

"I can't," she whispered.

He slipped an arm around her shoulders. "You can. I've got you."

Leaning into his embrace, she shuddered as the next roll of thunder cracked outside. It was quickly followed by the sound of the rising wind. He racked his mind for a way to comfort her. "Annie, remember the story in the Bible about Jesus walking across the water to the boat with His disciples in it?"

"Yes." Her voice was so small he almost couldn't hear it.

"When He asked Peter to come across the water to Him, what happened?"

"I don't remember."

"Yes, you do. Peter began walking on the water, but then he noticed the storm and he began to sink."

"Yes."

"Tell me what happened next. I know that you know."

"Jesus held out His hand and took hold of Peter."

"That's right. And what did He say to Peter?"

"Oh, ye of little faith. Why do you doubt me?"

"You aren't a woman of little faith, Annie."

She burrowed closer as the thunder rumbled again. "Sometimes I am."

"Okay, sometimes we all doubt, but not now. Say it. Say I'm a woman of strong faith."

"I'm a woman…of strong faith."

"Good. Now I'm going to pick you up and I'm going to carry you to the car outside."

"No."

"You'll get wet, that's all that will happen. I'm going to take care of you. Do you believe that? Open your eyes and look at me. Do you believe I'll keep you safe?"

She drew away from him enough to meet his gaze. "Yes."

"All right, then. Here we go." He stood and scooped her up in his arms. She wrapped her arms around his neck in a death grip.

He said, "Olivia, get the door. Here we go, Annie. I've got you."

She buried her face in his neck and whispered, "I'm a woman of strong faith."

"That's right. Just keep saying it."

"I'm a woman of strong faith. Oh, hurry."

He did just that, rushing down the steps to the waiting taxi, with Olivia carrying Annie's bag behind him. From the corner of his eye he saw Marge pull into the drive. At least now he didn't have to worry about leaving Olivia alone in the storm.

He placed Annie in the backseat and took her bag from Olivia. Marge came running up to stand beside him. Quickly he explained what they were doing and told Marge he would call when they got to Houston. After a quick hug from both mother and daughter, he climbed in beside Annie. She burrowed into his side as he gave the cabbie directions.

Twenty minutes later they were at the small commercial airstrip outside of town, where a twin-engine Cessna sat on the runway. The storm had moved on, leaving the tarmac gleaming with pockets of silver puddles glistening in the runway lights and the night air smelling freshly washed.

A crew of three met them at the door of the plane. A young man in a blue jumpsuit introduced himself as their flight nurse. After a few brief instructions, he settled Annie on the gurney and hooked her up to a small monitor. The steady bleep of her heart rate was all but drowned out by the engine noise as the pilot prepared for takeoff. After the nurse had Annie strapped in, he instructed Shane to take a nearby jump seat and then gave the all-clear to the pilot. Moments later the plane was airborne.

Once they stopped climbing, the nurse loosened Annie's straps and had her turn on her left side. She reached out, and Shane took her hand.

* * *

Shane's strong grip gave Annie a measure of peace as he squeezed her fingers in a gesture of reassurance. His determination gave her the strength she needed to nourish a small spark of hope.

"Thank you," she said, knowing the words were inadequate to express her gratitude for all he had done.

"You're welcome," he said with a soft smile full of love and understanding. "We'll be there in a couple of hours. Try and get some rest."

Annie closed her eyes, but she knew she wouldn't sleep. She kept one hand on her tummy, waiting for and rejoicing in each movement the baby made. When the baby slept for long periods without moving, Annie prayed.

Please, God, don't let it be too late. Please let this be the right decision.

Finally she felt the plane begin its descent. The young man in charge of her care made sure she was secure and then took his seat beside Shane. The plane touched down with a few hard bumps, then taxied along the runway to where an ambulance sat waiting.

Within minutes she found herself transferred into the waiting vehicle. Shane wasn't allowed to ride in back with her but had to sit with the driver. She missed the comfort his presence brought, but she knew she could make the rest of the journey alone if she had to. He believed she was strong. She would be for his sake. The pilot and her nurse wished her well as the door was being closed.

Annie realized that she didn't even know their names. It was humbling to know so many strangers were willing to help her and her child. The world might be full of pain and sorrow, but it was full of good people, too.

The ride to the medical center was uneventful. When the ambulance doors opened again, the bright lights and bustle of a busy emergency room surrounded her. As she was wheeled in through the hospital doors, she glanced back, trying to find Shane.

"We're taking you straight up to the obstetrical unit," the man pushing her bed told her as they passed out of the emergency room and into a long corridor.

"Where is Shane? The man who came with me."

"He's been shown to the admissions office. He'll be up when he gets finished with the paperwork and after they have you settled in your room on OB."

Annie nodded and tried to relax. Soon they would know if all of this effort had been for nothing. She wanted Shane beside her when she heard the doctor's report.

A flurry of activity greeted Annie when she reached her room. Nurses checked her vital signs and soon had her hooked up to a fetal monitor. The rapid beep-beep of her daughter's heartbeat was music to Annie's ears, but she caught the worried glance shared between two of the nurses.

"What is it?" Annie demanded.

"The baby's heart rate is a little too fast. We're calling for a stat echo. Dr. Wong will be here shortly."

There was nothing Annie could do but wait, worry and pray as the minutes dragged on.

Shane arrived just as the sonogram machine was being moved into the room. Intense relief at seeing him flooded her body and brought tears to her eyes. She blinked them back. It wasn't time for tears. Not yet.

Making his way around the people in the room, Shane reached her side and took hold of her hand. She brought it to her face and held it close. With his free hand he smoothed the hair back from her forehead and planted a kiss on her brow. Wordlessly they waited.

The sonogram technician had just started when a small Asian man in rumpled green scrubs came into the room, followed by a tall man with thick black-rimmed glasses. "What do we have?" the first one asked, taking the wand from the tech's hand and studying the image on the screen intently.

The nurse wrapping a blood-pressure cuff around Annie's arm said, "This is Dr. Wong and Dr Wilmeth."

"Hello, hello," Dr. Wong said, never taking his eyes from the screen. "I want to meet your baby first and then I'll talk to you. Ah, yes, it is a big mass. Even bigger than Dr. Merrick reported."

Dr. Wilmeth leaned over his shoulder. "This is not good."

"Can you save her?" Annie asked, squeezing Shane's hand tightly.

Dr. Wong looked up at his partner. "She's in trouble, but I think she has a chance if we go to surgery right away."

Pushing his glasses higher on his nose, Dr. Wilmeth said, "We can try. Do they know the risks?"

Dr. Wong handed the wand back to the technician waiting patiently at his side. "I've seen all I need. Get the rest of the measurements for me, please."

He pulled off his gloves with a snap and tossed them

into the trash can against the wall. "I want you to know that this is a very risky and delicate procedure. Many things can go wrong. It has only been done a handful of times. I can't guarantee anything."

"We understand that," Shane assured him.

"It will be major surgery for both of you," Dr. Wilmeth added. "The baby isn't mature enough to survive outside the womb. Even if the surgery is a success, there is a chance you will deliver prematurely and she will die anyway or suffer major repercussions such as blindness, cerebral palsy, deafness or seizures. Miss Delmar, the risks to you include bleeding, infection and the possibility that you won't be able to have other children. You must be prepared to spend weeks here being monitored around the clock and given drugs to halt any labor."

Annie looked at Shane. He would have to go back to Fort Riley and on to Germany in a few weeks. She would be in a strange city alone, without anyone to support her if the worst happened. How could she do it?

Shane pressed his lips together, then said, "It's your decision, Annie."

When had she ever made a good decision? Her life had been filled with mistakes and bad judgment. Now Shane was asking her to make the most important decision of all. "You think I can do this?"

"I know you can. Hey, you went out in a thunderstorm, didn't you?"

She managed a half smile. "That's right. What was I thinking? I'm practically Super Annie."

"Honey, you're the closest thing to a superhero I have ever met—and I've met some tough people."

"Okay." She called on every ounce of faith she possessed and prayed she was doing the right thing for her baby and herself. Turning her gaze back to Dr. Wong, she said, "I'm ready when you are. I will do whatever it takes."

"Are you sure you don't have any questions?"

"None," Shane said. "But I do need you to do me a favor. I need a paternity test done. The Army requires proof that this is my baby before she can be considered a dependent since Annie and I aren't married. And I'm told we need to speak to a social worker about getting Annie a medical card."

"Very well. Nurse, if you will get the consents signed and take care of notifying social work, I will notify the operating room. Oh, and get my usual labs stat and notify the blood bank that I want three units of packed cells on hold for this."

As the doctors and nurses filed out of the room, Annie found herself alone with Shane. He pulled a chair close to her bedside and sat down with a sigh.

"Are you tired?" She had been so concerned about herself that she hadn't given any thought to what he had been going through.

He wrinkled his nose. "A little."

"I'll trade you places and you can go get some sleep in surgery."

"On second thought, I'm not tired at all." He glanced at his watch. "It's only four-forty in the morning. In twenty minutes I will have been up for twenty-four hours."

A sudden thought struck Annie. "Shane, how did you get emergency leave so quickly? I'm not even your dependent."

"I'm not exactly on leave."

"You're AWOL? Shane!" She rose on her elbows to stare at him in shocked disbelief.

"I will be in twenty more minutes. Don't worry. Captain Watson is a stand-up guy. He'll understand and he'll do what he can for me."

"You'll be thrown in the brig. You'll be busted in rank. You won't get the promotion you've been working for."

"No, but I got to hold your hand for seven hundred miles. I think that's worth a night in the brig."

"Be serious. You could be in big trouble."

"Relax. I'm not going to be in big trouble. I promise. A little trouble, yes, but nothing I can't handle. They'll tell me to get back as soon as possible and I'll do that."

She sank back onto the bed. "You didn't have to come. I would have come alone if I had known you were risking a court-martial to be here."

He reached out and cupped her cheek. "I didn't *have* to be here, Annie. I *want* to be here. With you."

Covering his hand with her own, she closed her eyes and drew a quick breath. "I'm so glad you are. I'm so scared."

"Me, too, but we'll get through this together. You, me, the baby and God."

The door to the room opened again and two women in blue surgical garb pushed a narrow cart into the room. "We're here to take you to surgery, Miss Delmar. I have some papers for you to sign, but first I need to see your identification bracelet."

Shane stepped out of the way as Annie answered questions and signed the necessary papers. Another woman came in, pushing a cart loaded with lab tubes and needles, and announced that she had come to draw blood. She gave Shane a pointed look and asked him to step outside. As he pulled open the door, another nurse came in pushing an IV pump and carrying a tray. Knowing he was only in the way, he stepped out into the hallway.

He checked his watch as he waited, and when it hit five o'clock straight up, he pulled his cell phone from his pocket and dialed Captain Watson's number. When his captain picked up, Shane took a deep breath and said, "Sir, this is Corporal Ross. I'd like to report myself AWOL."

For a long second there was dead silence on the line. "I see. This is a very serious matter, Corporal."

"I understand that, but Annie and the baby need emergency care that is only available to them here in Houston. I want you to know I did attempt to contact you last night, but I was told you were unavailable."

"Yes, I spent a very boring evening with General Adams and his wife. However, that's no excuse, soldier."

"I wouldn't have done it if I felt there was any other choice. The baby will die unless they can do surgery on her tonight. She might die anyway, but we had to try."

"Of course. You'll have to report back by tomorrow at the latest, but I can't do anything for you if you're gone more than forty-eight hours. You do realize this is going on your record. I'll try to see that you get ten days emergency leave, but I'm not going to promise you anything."

"I understand, sir."

"All right. Let me know how the surgery turns out and when to expect you back."

The door to Annie's room opened and she was wheeled out into the hall.

"I will, sir. I have to go now."

"I'll be keeping you in my prayers, son."

"Thank you, sir. We need all we can get."

Shane snapped his phone shut and stepped up to the cart. One of the nurses had placed a blue surgical cap on Annie's head. She looked like a very frightened young woman trying to look brave for his benefit. It almost broke his heart.

Bending down, he placed a gentle kiss on her lips, then whispered, "See you soon."

She laid a hand on his cheek. "I love you, Corporal Shane Ross."

How he could love someone so much was a mystery to him. That she loved him in return was a blessing he would give thanks for all his life. "I love you, too."

One of the nurses said, "We have to go now. You can wait here in the room. Dr. Wong will find you when the surgery is over. If you leave, just let someone at the nurses' station know where you'll be. Try not to worry. We'll take good care of her."

As they pushed the cart down the hall, Shane watched until they rounded the corner and were lost from sight. Suddenly the energy drained out of his body, leaving him weak and vulnerable.

Pushing open the door to Annie's room, he walked in and sat down in the chair by her now-empty bed. A lump pushed up in his throat, making it hard to breathe. He leaned forward and braced his elbows on his knees, but he couldn't draw a full breath. He pressed his fingers against his stinging eyes, but it was no use.

A single sob escaped his tightly clenched lips, followed by another and then another. Defeated, he dropped his head into his hands and wept.

Many long hours later there was a knock at the door and Dr. Wong walked in.

Chapter Seventeen

Annie tried to open her eyes, but they wouldn't cooperate. She could hear voices near her, but she chose to ignore them. Sleep was a wonderful invention.

"Annie, open your eyes," someone insisted once more.

On the second try, Annie's lids fluttered up for a brief second before dropping closed again. Wasn't that good enough? Couldn't they just go away and let her sleep?

"Annie, wake up!" Recognizing the insistence in Shane's tone, she gave up the idea of ignoring him and opened her eyes. This time they stayed open and his face swam into view.

Annie smiled. He was so handsome and she loved him to pieces.

"That's a girl."

Little by little, the events of the past days fell into place. She had to try twice before she managed to croak out, "How is she?"

"She came though the surgery okay. They removed the tumor without complications."

Thank God. Joy filled her heart.

"Things look good," Shane said. The tension in his voice caused her to frown.

"But?"

"But I have to leave now. I have to catch the first flight back to Kansas City and get back to the base by tonight."

"Already? But we just got here." She wanted to make him smile. He looked so tired and worn.

"Yes, but I'll be back as soon as I can."

"When?" Annie cleared her throat and wished she could get a sip of water. It seemed like too much trouble to ask for it.

"I'm not sure."

"Do you get to make phone calls from the brig?" Her eyes drifted closed.

"I don't think so."

"Okay," she managed to say. "I'm going to go back to sleep now."

"That's a good thing. Sleep and get well—both of you."

She felt the butterfly-soft kiss he placed on her cheek and she drifted back to sleep, knowing she had made the right decision after all. Her baby was okay and Shane loved her. She managed to pry her eyes open one more time. Her strong man stood by her bed with tears running down his face.

"Don't cry."

"I'm sorry. I just don't want to leave you like this."

"We'll be here when you come back. Have faith. I do."

If he heard her barely whispered words, she didn't know it because sleep had claimed her once more.

* * *

Sitting up in her hospital bed, Annie surfed through the TV channels for the fifth time, and there still wasn't anything she wanted to watch. Soap operas, talk shows and action movies couldn't hold her interest the way the sound of her daughter's heartbeat did as it emanated softly from the monitor overhead. A tiny, fast, repetitive bleep proved all was well. It was a blessed sound.

Another contraction tightened Annie's stomach, and she winced at the pain, then took deep breaths to ride through the discomfort. She glanced at the nurse adjusting the IV drug on the pump beside her. "I don't think that one was quite as strong."

"Good, then the terbutaline is doing its job. I'll keep an eye on your strip from the desk. Let me know if they become more frequent or intense. Can I get you anything else?"

"No, thanks. You have all been so wonderful."

"We're just doing our job. But I have to admit it's exciting to be taking part in such a rare medical procedure. Your case has been discussed at length in our staff meetings. Everyone is praying that we can get your baby close to term."

"I'll be forty weeks the first of October. You will all be tired of me by then." Today was only the twenty-third of June.

"Once we get these contractions to stop and stay stopped, you'll be able to move off the floor into something more homey."

"Yes, the social worker has made arrangement with the Ronald McDonald House for me to stay there."

"I've heard it's really nice." The beeper in the nurse's pocket went off, and she excused herself as she walked out of the room.

Annie glanced out the window. Her room had a wonderful view of the brick wall of the building next door. The only amusement it afforded was the pigeons that strutted across the window ledges. Sighing, she picked up the remote again, but before she could turn it on, her door opened again.

"May I come in?"

"Shane!" she shrieked. Joy rocketed through her body. She sat up quick enough to make her incision hurt and had to grab her tummy with both hands.

"She sounds glad to see you," Olivia pushed past him and came bouncing into the room. "Surprise."

Wrapping her arms around the child, Annie gave her a heartfelt hug. "Olivia, oh, it's so good to see you. Where is your mother?"

"I'm right here," Marge said, smiling from the doorway beside Shane. She came forward, holding a large bouquet of yellow roses, and hugged Annie as Olivia plopped into the chair beside the bed.

With tears of happiness blurring her vision, Annie held out her hands to Shane. It was all the invitation he needed. He strode in and sat on the opposite side of her bed. For a long second he simply held her hands, then he leaned in and kissed her with fierce longing.

Blushing, but happier than she could imagine, Annie pulled away and cupped his face in her hands to drink in the sight of her beloved. "I missed you."

"I missed you, too. So much. How is our soccer player doing?" He laid his hand carefully on Annie's stomach.

"She's kicking one goal after another."

"Good for her."

"Can't you give the poor thing a name?" Olivia asked.

Annie and Shane exchanged sheepish looks. "We haven't discussed names," Annie said, squeezing his hands. Just touching him made her feel safe and loved. What a gift he was.

Olivia rolled her eyes. "Whatever you do, don't name her after me."

"What's wrong with your name?" Marge asked with a frown.

"She'll hate it when they call her Ollie for short. I do."

"We'll take that under advisement," Shane said.

Annie smiled at him. "I can't believe you brought them all this way. Thank you."

"Not!" Olivia said quickly. "We brought him. I didn't think Mom's clunker would make it this far, but it did."

Giving Shane a quizzical look, Annie said, "Why didn't you drive your own car?"

"I don't actually own a car anymore."

"What happened to your Mustang?"

"I sold it."

"Why? You love that car. Hey, *I* even love that car."

Shrugging, he said, "It was time for something different."

"I thought you sold it to pay for the air ambulance," Olivia interjected.

"Olivia Renee Lilly!" Marge said sternly.

"What did I do?"

Annie looked at Shane in disbelief. "You sold your car to get me here? Are you nuts? That car is going to be worth a fortune someday."

"What does a man need with a fortune someday when he has a pearl of great price sitting beside him?"

"Ooh, that was smooth, Shane." Olivia clapped her hands.

Marge stepped forward and laid a hand on her daughter's shoulder. "Excuse us, we're going to step out into the hall and give you two some privacy."

"But why?"

Glaring down at Olivia, Marge said, "Do you remember what used to happen when I had to take you out of church when you were little and misbehaving?"

Olivia's eye widened. "You wouldn't."

"Don't tempt me."

Olivia rose quickly and headed for the door. Marge looked at Annie. "We'll be back in a little while."

Olivia leaned back in from the door frame. "Yeah, he has something he wants to ask you."

Shane tilted his head to the side and glared at her. She waved and then popped out of sight.

Marge glanced toward the ceiling. "I'm trying, Lord. I know she is a test of patience, as well as a joy for my soul, but can You do something about her attitude before I decide to do a major readjustment?"

Annie had to laugh. "Marge, you know that kid is just like you."

Clutching her chest with one hand, Marge grimaced. "You wound me to the quick. But it's true. We'll be back in half an hour." Setting the vase of roses on the nightstand, she followed her daughter out of the room.

Happy to be alone with Shane, Annie reached up to stroke his cheek, then laced her fingers together at the nape of his neck. "I'm so glad you're here. I'm so glad we made this choice—no matter how it turns out."

"I am, too."

"What did you want to ask me?"

He looked down for a second and she sensed his unease. His eyes, when he looked at her again, were serious. A small frown creased his brow. "I have some news. My transfer has been bumped up. I'm leaving for Germany a week from today."

She bit her lip. "I thought we would have more time together."

"We'll have five whole days—and we'll make the most of them."

Don't cry. Be strong for him. "Okay. I can deal with that. Five days."

"I'm pretty sure I can get more leave once the baby is born. The paternity test proved that she is mine, and as my dependent, all her care will be covered by my military insurance."

"That's good. One less worry, right?"

"Right." He looked down again.

"Is there something else?"

"Yes. I was wondering if—if we could name her Clara, after my mother."

"Clara. Clara. That's a nice name. I like it."

"Thanks." He relaxed, but something in his attitude puzzled her.

"Dear, what's wrong?"

* * *

Shane drew a deep breath and pulled the small black box from his pants pocket. He held it tightly in his palm.

Please, God, I know that I've put this woman though immeasurable pain and suffering, but I love her. Please let her say yes.

Meeting Annie's gaze, he found the courage to offer it to her. "This isn't the time or the place I would have chosen, but I can't leave the country without knowing that we have a future together that is based on more than our child."

She opened the box. A silver band with a small diamond lay in the rich folds of satin. She pressed a hand to her lips. "Oh, Shane."

"I want you to be my wife. Annie Delmar, I love you with all my heart and soul. Will you marry me?"

For the longest moment she didn't say or do anything. Her eyes were wide with shock as she stared at him. Slowly her stunned expression gave way to the most beautiful smile he had ever beheld.

"Yes. Yes. Yes, yes, yes!" She threw her arms around his neck, then moaned and drew back and gripped her stomach in pain. "Oh, I forget I can't move that fast yet."

"Are you all right?"

She nodded as she grimaced. "I've never been happier in my life."

"Oh, Annie. I'm going to spend the rest of my life making this up to you."

"Good." She tried to laugh but couldn't. "I'll hold you to that."

Now that she had said yes, happiness fizzed through his

mind, making him giddy with relief and joy. "When can we get married? I want to do it before I have to leave you."

"You want me to plan a wedding in less than five days?"

"You can't do it?"

She leaned back in the bed. "You're talking to Super Annie. Of course I can do it. How soon can you get Pastor Hill here?"

"My friend Avery has this great souped-up Mustang Mach One. I think he can have the pastor here in about eight hours."

"Saturday will be soon enough. You'll need to get a marriage license. Find Marge and send her in. She's going to have to find me a wedding dress. I refuse to get married in a hospital gown."

She pressed both hands to her cheeks. "Oh, my stars. Is this real?"

"As real as this." He leaned in and kissed her soundly.

On Saturday afternoon Annie, dressed in a simple white taffeta dress with a rounded neck and capped sleeves, sat in a wheelchair at the back of the hospital's small chapel and smoothed the pink sash that rested just above her bulging tummy. She couldn't tell if it was just nervous butterflies or if her little soccer player had taken up gymnastics. She looked down at her feet. The rhinestone-covered sandals had been borrowed from Olivia at the girl's insistence. After all, no one could get married in hospital slippers.

Shane and Avery, in their dress uniforms, stood beside Pastor Hill at the front of the chapel. The few rows of pews were filled with OB nurses, surgical staff and even Dr. Wilmeth and Dr. Wong.

"Are you ready?" Marge, dressed in a powder-blue suit, waited at Annie's side.

"I was just wishing that my parents could be here. I wish my dad were walking me down the aisle."

"You should have called them."

"There wasn't time, and I'm not sure they would have come anyway. No, I'm okay. We don't dwell on past mistakes. We dwell in the present and go forward from here."

She smiled at Marge as she stood up and stepped away from her wheelchair. "I'm ready. My future is standing there waiting for me, and I love him more than life itself. God has been good to me."

Epilogue

Annie gazed with love at the small bundle in her arms. Sitting up in bed the day after her C-section, she still couldn't get over how beautiful her daughter was. Her thick black hair stood on end and refused to lie down no matter how much the nurses tried combing it or how much lotion they applied.

Clara's little bow mouth was busy making sucking motions as she dreamed of her next meal. Even though her eyes were closed, Annie knew they were the same bright blue as her father's.

Annie glanced at the clock on the wall. According to the Red Cross volunteer who had called earlier, Shane should be arriving about five o'clock. It was a quarter to five now. Shane would be here any minute. She could barely contain her excitement. The long months of waiting were finally over. Clara Olivia Ross had entered the world three weeks early but in perfect health, at five pounds three ounces and with a squall that would wake anyone within half a mile.

A new nurse came in and stopped at the bedside. "I'm here to take your vital signs, Mrs. Ross. How are you feeling?"

"Wonderful." She ran her fingers though Clara's downy hair and smiled.

"Good. I'm going to give you a bath demonstration in a little while, but I'd like your husband to be here for that."

"He's on his way. His flight should have landed an hour ago."

"Oh, he hasn't seen the baby yet?"

"No, she showed up early and spoiled our plans for him to be here. She's had a way of messing with our lives from the get-go."

"What does your husband do?"

Clara stirred and thrust one hand in the air. Annie caught it and thrilled to the strength of her baby's grip. She bent and placed a kiss on the tiny fingers curled around her own. "You have a military daddy, don't you, Clara?" she cooed.

The door opened and Shane rushed in. His uniform was rumpled, and he looked as tired as a man who had been on a plane or in airports for the last twenty hours. He dropped his duffel bag off his shoulder and walked with unsteady steps toward Annie.

Smiling through tears of joy, Annie said, "Daddy, someone wants to welcome you home." She held the baby out to him.

The look of love and wonder on his face as he took his daughter and held her close was something that Annie knew she would always remember and treasure.

"She's so beautiful." He raised his eyes to Annie. "She looks like her mother."

"But she has her father's charm."

Shane leaned in to kiss Annie—for a moment everything faded except for the feel of his lips on hers.

He pulled back and reached out to touch her face. "How are you?"

"I'm fine. Welcome home."

"I can't believe she is finally here. She's perfect, Annie, just perfect."

"Yes, she's a pure and simple gift from God."

"Oh, I almost forgot." He grinned at Annie and gave the baby back to her. "I brought you both something. Marge and Pastor Hill had been doing a little detective work for me. I had a four-hour layover in New York, so I took the ferry out to Long Island. Look what I found there."

He pulled open the door and motioned to someone in the hall. "Come in. Come and meet your granddaughter."

Stunned into speechlessness, Annie watched as her mother and father walked cautiously into the hospital room.

They were so much older than she remembered. Had she aged them that much?

Her mother spoke first. "Hello, Annie." She pressed a hand to her lips. "Oh, my, she is a pretty baby."

Walking up to stand beside his wife, her father thrust his hands in his pockets. "She looks a lot like you did the day you were born, Annie." His voice cracked with emotion and he wiped at his eyes.

Annie laid her daughter down carefully on the bed in front of her. "I can't believe you are here."

Her mother sniffed and nodded. "Shane has told us about all you've been though. I'm so grateful that you've been able to turn your life around. I've prayed for this day."

"And I'm so sorry for all that I put you through. Can you ever forgive me?" She held out her arms and found herself enveloped in her mother's embrace. A second later her father threw his arms around both of them. The tears they shed as they clung to one another washed years of bitterness and sorrow away.

From his place at the foot of the bed Shane looked on through tears of his own. His wife and his daughter were safe and he was with them. God was good.

* * * * *

Be sure to read Patricia Davids's next military story,
A Military Match,
available in November 2008.

Dear Reader,

Thank you for reading *Military Daddy,* my second book about a member of the Commanding General's Mounted Color Guard at Fort Riley, Kansas. I hope you enjoyed it. The men, women and horses of the unit have won a special place in my heart with their authentic recreation of the U.S. Cavalry in the 1800s. I'd like to extend my thanks again to the Fort Riley Department of Public Affairs and the members of CGMCG for their help while I was researching this story.

My heroine, Annie, like millions of people around the world, suffers from alcoholism. It is a disease that has left few families untouched by the sorrow it brings. Annie, like many alcoholics, found help in Alcoholics Anonymous. AA has enabled thousands upon thousands of people to live full, productive, sober lives. God bless them for the work they do.

I always enjoy hearing from people who have read my stories. You may contact me by e-mail at pat@patriciadavids.com or you may write to me at P.O. Box 16714, Wichita, Kansas 67216.

Blessings,

Patricia Davids

QUESTIONS FOR DISCUSSION

1. When Annie tells Shane that she is pregnant, he is confronted with a choice about how deeply involved he should be. Why do you think he was so determined to be a true father? Do you know someone who made a different choice than the one Shane made?

2. Shane tried to convince Annie that he is earnest about being a part of his child's life. She is reluctant to accept that his intentions are sincere. Have you been suspicious of someone's motivation when they offered help to you? Do you choose to see the best or the worst in people? Discuss.

3. Annie is determined to make it on her own. Have you rejected help because of pride? When is it okay to admit you can't go it alone?

4. Annie struggled to live a sober life. She has failed more than once but continues to try. Do you know anyone struggling with addiction? Which means more to you, that they fail or that they try again? What can be done to help them?

5. Marge opens her home to young women in dire circumstances. In your community, what can you do to help people like Annie and Crystal?

6. When Annie learns Olivia has been drinking, she sees

her own unhappy past. She wants to help the child avoid the mistakes she made. What role does our faith play when we are confronted with a child who strays from the path?

7. After Shane sees how faith in God has helped Annie and others at AA, he is inspired to seek God for himself. What event or events led you to seek the Lord?

8. Shane is delighted when Annie says that she will allow him to be involved in their baby's life, but he finds himself wanting more. He wants a relationship with Annie. When has God granted you what you desired and yet you found yourself wanting more from Him? Is there a limit to what we may ask God to do for us?

9. Annie is devastated when she learns about her baby's birth defect. She feels abandoned by God. Her faith wavers and she thinks that God is punishing her for the sins she committed. Have you ever felt punished or abandoned by God? How did you overcome it?

10. Annie must trust Shane to help her overcome her doubts and fears. Shane's strong new faith in God helps Annie to recover her trust in the Lord. Have you known "new converts" who seemed to have greater faith than some that have "grown up" in the church? Why do you think that is?

11. Annie has to make a decision to try and save her baby that could put her own life at risk. What big decision

have you faced in your life that had no clear-cut answer? Did you find the courage to overcome your fears and put the situation in God's hands or did you try to "fix it" yourself? Discuss.

12. Annie's friend Crystal was hiding the fact that she had started drinking again. When she sees Annie's despair, she offers Annie a bottle. Why do you think Crystal did that? Have you ever been tempted by something you know is bad for you? How has God helped you resist temptation?

13. Crystal's future is left undisclosed in this story. What do you think her future is and why? Do you know someone who seemed to be on the right path but faltered? How can you help people who lose their way?

14. Annie and Shane are blessed with a healthy baby when their child is born. How much more difficult is it to see God's love when a child is born with a handicap? Have you or someone you know faced this challenge? How has it affected your faith?

REQUEST YOUR FREE BOOKS!

2 FREE INSPIRATIONAL NOVELS
PLUS 2
FREE
MYSTERY GIFTS

YES! Please send me 2 FREE Love Inspired® novels and my 2 FREE mystery gifts (gifts are worth about $10). After receiving them, if I don't wish to receive any more books, I can return the shipping statement marked "cancel". If I don't cancel, I will receive 4 brand-new novels every month and be billed just $4.24 per book in the U.S. or $4.74 per book in Canada, plus 25¢ shipping and handling per book and applicable taxes, if any*. That's a savings of over 20% off the cover price! I understand that accepting the 2 free books and gifts places me under no obligation to buy anything. I can always return a shipment and cancel at any time. Even if I never buy another book, the two free books and gifts are mine to keep forever.

113 IDN ERXA 313 IDN ERWX

Name	(PLEASE PRINT)	
Address		Apt. #
City	State/Prov.	Zip/Postal Code

Signature (if under 18, a parent or guardian must sign)

Order online at www.LoveInspiredBooks.com
Or mail to Steeple Hill Reader Service:
IN U.S.A.: P.O. Box 1867, Buffalo, NY 14240-1867
IN CANADA: P.O. Box 609, Fort Erie, Ontario L2A 5X3

Not valid to current subscribers of Love Inspired books.

Want to try two free books from another series?
Call 1-800-873-8635 or visit www.morefreebooks.com

* Terms and prices subject to change without notice. N.Y. residents add applicable sales tax. Canadian residents will be charged applicable provincial taxes and GST. This offer is limited to one order per household. All orders subject to approval. Credit or debit balances in a customer's account(s) may be offset by any other outstanding balance owed by or to the customer. Please allow 4 to 6 weeks for delivery. Offer available while quantities last.

Your Privacy: Steeple Hill Books is committed to protecting your privacy. Our Privacy Policy is available online at www.SteepleHill.com or upon request from the Reader Service. From time to time we make our lists of customers available to reputable third parties who may have a product or service of interest to you. If you would prefer we not share your name and address, please check here. ☐

LIREG08

TITLES AVAILABLE NEXT MONTH

Don't miss these four stories in May

TO LOVE AGAIN by Bonnie K. Winn
A Rosewood, Texas novel

Laura Manning moved her family to Rosewood to take over her late husband's share of a real-estate firm. Who was Paul Russell to tell her she couldn't? She'd prove to the handsome Texan that she could do anything.

A SOLDIER'S HEART by Marta Perry
The Flanagans

After wounded army officer Luke Marino was sent home, he refused physical therapy. But Mary Kate Flanagan Donnelly needed Luke's case to prove herself a capable therapist. If only it wasn't so hard to keep matters strictly business...

MOM IN THE MIDDLE by Mae Nunn
Texas Treasures

Juggling caring for her son and elderly parents kept widow Abby Cramer busy. Then her mother broke her hip at a store. Good thing store employee Guy Hardy rushed in to save the day with his tender kindness toward her whole family—especially Abby herself.

HOME SWEET TEXAS by Sharon Gillenwater

When a strange man appeared to her like a mirage in the desert, he was the answer to the lost and injured woman's prayers. But she couldn't tell her handsome rescuer, Jake Trayner, who she was. Because she couldn't remember....

LICNM0408